Eastbound Sailing

a novel by

Todd Foley

Cedar Rock Publishers

Eastbound Sailing

Published by Cedar Rock Publishers.

ISBN: 978-0-9880417-0-7 (paperback).

Printed in the United States of America. Registered with Library and Archives Canada.

Cover art by Daniel Sicolo (www.danielsicolo.com).

Connect with Todd on Twitter @tdiddy1234 or at Scribbledrevisions.com.

The following story is entirely fictional.

DEDICATION

To my parents for enabling me to risk, fail and try
again.
To Mrs. Simpson for teaching me to love literature.
To Fred D. for teaching me to cut text mercilessly.
To Cecilia B. for holding me accountable in completing
this project.
To Fred B. for helping me rework my thoughts into
cohesive sentences.
To my beautiful wife Kristen for being my much-
needed cheerleader along the way.
Finally, to Gram, my maternal grandmother, for
recognizing the writer in me.

CONTENTS

PART I

1. Embarkment   Pg 10

2. First Impressions, Again   Pg 16

3. Deflation, Direction   Pg 23

4. A Graceful Interruption   Pg 28

5. Lost Persona   Pg 38

6. Memory's Dock   Pg 46

7. Point Of Reference   Pg 52

8. Exposure   Pg 60

9. Assessed Value   Pg 63

10. Shame   Pg 66

11. Decision Points   Pg 71

12. Mockingbird   Pg 77

13. Markets, Freedoms   Pg 80

14. Old Souls Speak   Pg 89

15. The Exchange   Pg 99

16. Whispers from Parchments Past   Pg 105

17. Confessions After Midnight   Pg 111

18. Providence Realized   Pg 117

PART II

19. First Fruits   Pg 124

20. Pick Your Team   Pg 131

21. Stray   Pg 136

22. Three Voices   Pg 143

23. Loosened Stitch   Pg 154

24. Dear Dad   Pg 163

25. Inventory   Pg 169

26. Joint Venture   Pg 174

27. Harvesting Fate   Pg 182

PART III

28. Eager But For Daylight   Pg 186

29. A Wretch Like Me   Pg 189

30. Go East, Young Man   Pg 195

31. Sailing Against Sunrise   Pg 199

AUTHOR'S NOTE

Aiden Lawrence is fictional, but he's **real**.
Cielo Island doesn't exist, but it's **true**.
This story may seem hopeless, but it points to **hope**.
It's **human**.
That's what we are, and **we all need hope**.

PART I

1. EMBARKMENT

Aiden Lawrence never did like public transit. He rode a fair amount in his young life. Subways, buses, taxis. Regardless of the form, it tended to be overcrowded, uncomfortable and unpleasantly aromatic. And for some unknown reason, it brought with it a sense of anxiety.

He didn't recall ferries being that different. His dad took him on one to Cielo Island for his 13th birthday, a father-son excursion to their summer cabin, though they rarely took summer trips there. Mom was wheelchair-bound, hated the effort it took to get to the island and preferred to stay in their West Seattle home.

"We're leaving mainland America and heading to another world," Dad had said, trying to ease the anxious teen. *"Not so much a foreign universe, but a place of time passed."*

The visit to the small Pacific Northwest island wasn't so great, and neither was that first boat ride. Driving his '96 Civic hatchback onto the ferry 17 years later, the thrill was still missing.

"Don't worry, Aiden," Dad had said. *"Simply ride."*

Thrill was missing from life in general. A mature university student who dropped out three quarters of the way through his business degree from burn-out and apathy.

"Welcome aboard Washington State Ferries," the PA announced.

He was moving to the cabin for four months. Tentatively. Being out of school, timelines didn't play that prominent of a role anymore. Not much did, for that matter.

Aiden turned off the engine, locked the door and headed upstairs to the passenger area.

These boats were nothing exceptional: the white paint was rusted; the linoleum floor tiles were chipped; the seat cushions were faded; the vending machines offered snacks of little substance at a ridiculous price.

His cup of drip coffee was empty and ready to be discarded, and its contents had quickly made its way through his stomach. Once he walked into the bathroom, the aromas of public transit hit a new high. The smell does little to relax the soul – or ease your body to do what you came for.

Washed his hands, splashed some lukewarm water on his face, looked in the mirror. The 4 o'clock shadow was starting to show. Hadn't washed his dirty blond hair in a few days; it framed his boyish face and dark green eyes.

But it's not a baby face. Life has a way of stripping away innocent composition.

"Finally, I don't look like I'm 12," he thought to himself.

After holding his hands under the air dryer for 15 seconds – more so for heat – Aiden exited the bathroom and looked around. Lots of people. Families with children. Loud, rowdy children. Couples, old and young. Some were far too comfortable showing physical affection. Others sat with their books hardly acknowledging their partner. He found a booth, but kids kept running by, shouting as they dashed. It felt crowded.

Congested.

Threatening.

Aiden was taken back to that first trip with Dad, complaining about the boat. *"That's just the problem, Aiden,"* he had said. *"The boat isn't the attraction."*

Dads have a way of being right, even when it's not what one wants to hear.

Side by side, the father and son walked down the side to the outside deck.

"Welcome to heaven," Dad had said.

Through with recollection, Aiden grunted, buttoned up his faded grey blazer and walked to the set of push-doors.

The salty air blasted at his eyes and through his scruffy hair, quickly reminding him that he was far away from his Seattle suburb. There were few clouds in the sky. They looked just like the ones from back home, but the geographical similarities stopped there. No pavement. No smog. Just air. Crisp, moist air blanketed over the islands and water.

Aiden was always fascinated by salt water, an entire ecosystem that can sustain so many forms of life and yet corrode anything that lives outside of it. When a gust of wind hits the surface, the mist is carried high, gracing the sides of passing boats.

The faded paint on the ferry had a bit more meaning now. Faded and jaded over the years.

Felt familiar.

He gripped his hands around the green rail that bordered the small standing area.

This paint was also starting to chip away.

"Stop looking around and analyzing everything, Aiden," Dad would've said now. *"Just close your eyes."*

Aiden hated advice. Even when given out of love and care, advice carried with it stinging sentiments of inadequacy and inferiority – at least that's how he received it, and he let it fuel his self-doubt.

He valued wisdom from people who lived full lives. Growing up, he discovered a love for classic literature – works by F. Scott Fitzgerald, John Steinbeck, Jane Austen. Universal truths lived out by timeless characters – characters who experienced love and loss, passion and apathy. They taught by experience.

Advice, on the other hand, felt like a performance review – especially when it came from Dad. And in Aiden's eyes, those reviews rarely felt favorable. Being an only child brought with it extra expectations and pressures. Most times he threw them back in Dad's face.

He'd been living with regret since Dad died last year, and his hiatus from school felt more indefinite with each passing month.

What harm can a little advice do now?

He closed his eyes.

The predominate sound was the cold wind racing past his ears. Abrupt and loud.

"Listen," Dad would say.

He listened intently, and heard the head of the boat tearing through the water; he even felt a faint mist hit his face. Suddenly, the loudness wasn't harsh; it was refreshing.

He hadn't heard this sound in quite some time, at least not in the suburbs. He was used to loud noises caused by cars, subways, music and voices.

Not here. None of that was here.

Aiden opened his eyes.

His vision took a few minutes to adjust. Even though it was a cloudy day, the sky's light reflected off the water, naturally brightening up the day through his perspective.

For the moment, everything looked green and blue. Smeared, yet maintaining the distinct colors. As his eyes focused, the green separated from the blue. He noticed trees, ocean and sky. Then he noticed the rocks separating the trees from the shoreline.

Individual islands became recognizable. Homes were scattered across the edges of the shoreline. Some lavish, some rather modest in size.

"No property like this could be considered modest," he told himself.

Sad how Aiden remained so analytical even in these surroundings. Thinking through the details so much over the years made him lose his sense of wonder. Almost as much as the unexpected turns he came across in life.

Maybe the absence of wonder caused those turns.

Maybe the turns weren't so bad after all.

Maybe they could have turned for the better.

Maybe –

"May I have your attention please. We are now arriving at Cielo Island. Car drivers, please return to your vehicles. Foot passengers will disembark from the car deck. Please make sure you have all of your personal belongings."

He snapped back to reality. Not too far in the distance, he spotted the Cielo ferry landing. It's a small operation, with a few tall pilings – Dad called them "dolphins" – that guide the boat to its secure landing spot.

Aiden looked down at his hands, which hadn't loosened their grip on the green rail since he first stepped out on the deck. He let go and noticed some paint chips on his palms. Brushed them off.

He made his way down to the car deck. Down the stairs, not holding the hand rail. Too many people use this rail; who knew if any of those kids washed their hands.

He walked over to the Civic, unlocked the door and climbed in. He glance up at the ferry landing and noticed a large green arch; hanging from the top of that arch was a faded wooden sign that read "Cielo Island."

A small concrete ramp hung over the water supported by beams. A painted wooden building that served as a passenger waiting area, the size of an average office. Adjacent to that waiting area was a small convenience stand, selling fatty snacks and canned soda.

His engine revved up, and the friendly ferry workers gave him his cue: Aiden was free to drive off the boat.

"So it begins," he thought.

2. FIRST IMPRESSIONS, AGAIN

First impressions stick.

When he first came to Cielo for his 13th birthday, Aiden was disappointed by the scenery. Growing up in the city, island life was perceived as tropical and exotic. Palm trees, white sand, clear water.

Ceilo was merely rural. Nothing exotic.

Vast greenery bordered the paved road he was now driving down. Evergreen trees, firs, cedars and ferns. Every now and then some wildlife popped up. Rabbits, mainly, and the occasional deer.

He looked to the left for a street sign indicating the name of the road. After a quarter mile, he saw one that read "Canoe Drive." Cute.

Aiden's second visit to Cielo – he had referred to it as a "God-forsaken rock" – started off with the same level of excitement. The road winded through the greenery, then opened up to the countryside. Vast fields, scattered with cows and lambs, and occasional horses. The livestock don't run on a schedule and they have nowhere to be. They simply graze, sleep and meander. They exist in community.

Simple, Aiden thought. Too simple.

A large farm house stood on the right side of the road. Two stories, wooden frame, painted grey. It had a covered porch with no furniture other than a small clay flower pot; the begonias looked like they were starting to wilt.

Most homes in the country are on farm property. Some farms have livestock ranging from cattle and horses to pigs and lambs; others are strictly agricultural, a place where nurtured soil can produce a harvest of vegetables.

He got his focus back and kept his eyes peeled for the landmark that he and Dad searched for 17 years ago: Scarlet Lane.

After driving a few more miles, he spotted the street sign and turned left onto the small dirt road that went up a modest hill clouted with cedar trees. At the top of this hill was Dad's log cabin.

Strange how it almost seemed like yesterday that he first pulled into this driveway. The cabin itself was relatively small, a simple two-story structure, roughly 500 square feet with a small covered deck. At age 13, it felt like a castle. Maybe more of a fortress. Castles evoked feelings of wonder and adventure; fortresses felt like prisons, and Aiden was held captive. Not by force, just discontentment. He didn't like drastic change. Staring at the cabin through the windshield, he felt the same sentiment.

Aiden got out of the car, looked around and noticed that the half-acre property was equally modest. The surrounding cedar trees sheltered the cabin from storms, but also from the sun. A lone maple tree just to the left of the porch showed that September was indeed coming to an end, as a few brown leaves graced the driveway.

"Showing its age more and more," Aiden said under his breath as he surveyed the property.

He pulled his hands out of his jean pockets, walked to the Civic, pulled out his duffle bag and made his way to the front door. The one detail he distinctly recalled was that the key was hidden under a loose floor board beneath the hand rail. Kicked up the board, pulled out the key and opened the door.

The small area room had a couch and a chair next to the wood stove in the far left corner. The adjacent wall had a step ladder that led up to the sleeping area. A small kitchenette was set in the opposite corner of the ground level. Surprisingly, the cabin didn't smell too musty.

Aiden didn't have to open the cabinet to know there was no food. Hungry as he was, he had no interest in looking around the cabin and reminiscing, so he dropped his bag, grabbed his keys and started up the car. Time to go grocery shopping.

He got back in the car, drove down the dirt road and turned onto Canoe Drive. The road continued through farm land and eventually curved south along the ocean, bordering the shoreline for several miles. The sun was beginning to set in front, casting an orange hue across the water that reflected back to the clouds.

Aiden rolled down the window. For some reason he felt drawn to the salty scent he rediscovered on the ferry ride.

There it was again.

Refreshing.

Just over the crest of the hill, he saw the town — the commercial hub of the island. Not much more was needed for a population of 3,000. To Aiden it all felt so foreign.

Maybe that wasn't such a bad thing, all things considered.

Canoe Drive continued on past the town so Aiden hung a left onto Borough Boulevard.

That was it – the town is known to locals as the Borough, Dad had said.

It was coming back to him.

Slowly.

The main drag through town was bordered with small trees. Condos, homes, small businesses, studios and restaurants. Then he spotted the grocery store. All he really needed at this point.

Aiden parked the car in the small lot, got out and locked the doors.

"You're not from around here, are you," came a deep voice from behind him.

Aiden turned around and saw a tall man getting in a grey pickup truck.

"Beg your pardon?"

"You locked your car," the stranger said. "Nobody locks their cars here."

"I just got here today," Aiden responded, "still getting used to 'the island way.'"

The stranger rolled his eyes to the side. "Fearful mainlanders always lock their cars and look over their shoulders. They've got a stressed-out mentality when they come here."

Aiden was taken back by this guy's brashness – his first encounter with an islander in over 17 years.

He couldn't think of a response before the stranger shut the driver-side door and drove away.

So much for island hospitality, Aiden thought.

Even in a safe island community like Cielo, he lacked the trust to leave his car unlocked.

Not out of prejudice or anything personal against the island culture itself; he had just developed street smarts over the years.

Aiden would rather lack direction than walk through life blindly, as it seemed the locals did so carelessly.

At times, it struck Aiden how trust was lacking in most areas of life. Be it personal security, romantic relationships and even platonic friendships.

Even when it came to a beat-up Civic with nothing valuable inside apart from McDonalds coupons and a few CDs.

He couldn't bring himself to care, so he walked through the store's automatic double-door entrance, picked up a shopping basket and made the rounds. At this point all Aiden really cared about was dinner so he started at the meat and produce sections. He picked up a sirloin steak, a handful of mushrooms, a couple bell peppers and potatoes. There were some fresh herbs on sale, and he picked up thyme and basil.

Rounded the corner and found the spirits aisle. Scanned the wine selection and noticed a local section, with "Cielo Vineyards" gracing the matte label. He chose a bottle of merlot.

Aiden may have lost his sense of trust and wonder but he picked up a sense of taste.

Cooking gourmet meals was his creative outlet. Thanks to Dad's inheritance, Aiden pursued that hobby more through an increased grocery budget, meaning more alcohol for cooking. Wine has a way of drawing flavor out of anything it comes in contact with.

Following Dad's death, though, alcohol was a side-effect of Aiden's deepening apathy and depression. He didn't care to fight the cravings.

He grabbed a second bottle off the shelf.

While the Borough was far more subdued than the city life Aiden was used to, it did guarantee short check-out lines. He walked up to the cashier and placed the groceries on the conveyor belt. The cashier, a lady who looked to be in her 50s, scanned the items.

Quick and painless.

"$52 even, please."

So much for painless.

"$52? For just these groceries?" Aiden asked in shock.

"Yes, sir. The bottles are $18 each, the steak $6 and the produce comes to $10."

"Isn't that a little steep for produce?" he asked.

"Not when you buy local," the cashier responded. She looked Aiden in the eye, then softened her gaze.

"You're not from around here, are you?"

"You're the second person to ask that in the last 10 minutes," he said.

"Sorry, not trying to pry," she said. "Just a little insight into how things work around here: a box of local produce isn't just a box of produce. This is the heart and soul of the farmer. Time and energy are poured into the craft."

Here comes the hippie island rhetoric, Aiden grumbled to himself. "So I've heard. It's 'green,' I get it. It's just steep price to pay for a meal."

She held his eyes with hers. "You consider yourself an investor?"

Aiden didn't have time for this; his rolling eyes made that clear.

"I like to make my money count, and I enjoy quality. That what you're looking for?"

The cashier, seeming to have lots of time on her hands, went on. "Islanders live...they live within the environment, for lack of a simpler phrase." She spoke gently, but with conviction. "People invest themselves deeply into bringing out the best of the island, be it farming, construction, painting, cooking – you name it. When the island's at its best, nothing can compare with its beauty. But if neglected or poorly attended to, the island loses its luster. It becomes barren."

Aiden struggled to connect the dots, but he pressed on. He may get socially withdrawn from friends and family, but dialog with strangers was something he could handle.

"I'm failing to see the connection between a 'barren wasteland of an island' and overpriced groceries," he said.

She looked at him again with the same relaxed but strong expression. "That's what happens when we start importing cheap crap from the mainland. Like it or leave it. That's just how things are on Cielo."

"Well Granola it is," Aiden responded with a mix of sarcasm and disdain. He gave her his Visa card, signed the receipt and turned toward the exit. If his first two interactions were any indication, idle hands aren't the devil's playthings but rather a state of being on Cielo.

3. DEFLATION, DIRECTION

Canoe drive felt different when driving east. Aiden couldn't pin down whether it was the sights, the sounds or the pavement itself.

Whatever it was, it was quickly overshadowed as the passenger side of the car dipped down and a respective grinding noise grew louder.

Flat tire, he realized, slamming his right hand against the well-worn steering wheel.

He pulled to the side of the road, got out of the car and surveyed the damage. A broken bottle 20 feet back, and a deflated passenger-side tire.

He kicked the tire and swore. No spare tire in the back. Less than a quarter mile out of the Borough, Aiden's annoyance hit an even higher level.

Not only did he not want to be on this island, but now he was stranded in the countryside.

Aiden started walking back to the town, past a few homes and farms. His eyes remained on the road rather than the surroundings. His walk had a single destination; scenery would only deter him from getting back to some solitude.

When he reached the Borough 10 minutes later, he went back into the grocery store.

"Back for more?" the cashier asked, cleaning off the register with a faded blue cloth.

"Dont even get me started," Aiden thought to himself. He wasn't interested in conversation. Just wanted some direction.

"Flat tire, no spare," he said. No other words were needed. He didn't care to offer a nosey islander further insight into his life or circumstances.

"Ah," she said. "You'll want to head over to Dwayne's."

"Dwayne's?"

"Mechanic down the road. We can hold your food here in the fridge."

Aiden cursed to himself. After the head ache of buying the overpriced food, it was now going to waste in his car.

"You need a ride to pick it up and bring it back here?" the cashier asked, pointing at a nearby teenage boy. Store employee, Aiden guessed given the black apron. The boy didn't appear especially happy at the suggestion.

"Forget it, I just want my tire fixed."

"You've got a free ride here," she said.

"I didn't ask for charity."

"Then consider it product insurance," the old woman retorted. "Plus, you'll get to Dwayne's faster than you would on foot."

At this point, efficiency was Aiden's best friend, so he accepted.

He followed the young worker through the double-door entrance toward a green Jetta.

Couldn't be older than five years, Aiden thought, shocked that a 16-year-old on Cielo would have this nice of a ride.

"Your parents' car?" Aiden asked as he opened the passenger door.

"Nope, mine."

"A job at the store pays that well?" he asked.

"I saved. Not much to spend your money on here," the boy said.

They rode in silence for the rest of the short drive to Aiden's car. Neither of them wanted to shoot the breeze.

The Jetta stopped in the middle of the road, parallel to the Civic. Aiden hopped out and retrieved the bag of food as the Jetta did a quick U-turn, got back in and then they were off.

"I'll take it in," the boy said, reaching for the plastic bag as they pulled into the store lot.

"Where's the mechanic?" Aiden asked.

"Down the Boulevard one block south, hang a left at Harbor View. Dwayne's is the last building on the right."

Aiden gave a slight nod of acknowledgment as the boy walked away.

Five minutes later, he spotted an average-size concrete building, white and blue with the words "Dwayne's Mechanical Services" painted above the double garage opening.

An overalls-clad man – whom Aiden guessed to be in his 40s – walked out of the right-hand garage. Had to be Dwayne.

"You look stranded, son," he said, wiping grime off his hands with an oil-stained rag.

"Good call, Sherlock," Aiden thought to himself.

"Blew a tire just outside the town. No spare," he finally said. "How much to tow?"

"Nodda, we'll fix it on site. What do you drive?"

"95 Civic."

"$150 including a spare," Dwayne said, stuffing the rag in his back pocket.

Aiden was expecting far more; this was the first bit of good news today.

"Not bad," he admitted. "You want me to come with?"

"Yup."

They settled the payment in Dwayne's small cluttered office, and with that, Dwayne fired up a company truck and Aiden jumped in.

"You from out of town?" Dwayne asked, eyes on the road.

"Seattle."

"What brings you here?"

"Taking care of business," Aiden said, looking out the window.

Dwayne didn't prod, just drove.

They pulled up behind the Civic. Aiden unlocked the hatch, grabbed the jack and proceeded to raise the car high enough to remove the lug nuts. Dwayne had the tire down and ready to go just after the flat tire was off.

"What'd you hit?" he asked as he placed the new tire on the rim and tightened the lugs.

"Broken bottle," Aiden said. "Wouldn't kill people to pick up their crap."

"Wouldn't kill you to watch the road," the mechanic replied. "We don't have the luxury of street sweepers here."

Aiden had had just about enough criticism for one day. It was as if he had "ignorant outsider" stamped across his forehead. He hadn't the energy to continue the banter.

The tire was switched within minutes. Dwayne threw the flat in the truck and hopped in the driver seat.

"Watch the roads on your way home," he said. "You know where to come if you run into any problems. Tires have lifetime guarantee."

"Thanks," Aiden said insincerely. He put the spare in the back, started the engine and headed back to the store to pick up his groceries.

The cashier had his bag out on the counter, as if she was anticipating the time of his return to the second.

"Bon appetit," she said, holding the bag out to him.

Aiden pictured himself on Disneyland's "It's A Small Small World" ride, with the islanders' faces plastered on the demon-possessed dolls.

"Good timing," he said. Couldn't think of anything wittier to say. Didn't care to. She had pointed him to the resources he needed, so he at least owed her some gratitude.

"Thanks," he said as he walked out the double doors.

4. A GRACEFUL INTERUPTION

Aiden fired up the gas stove as soon as he got back to cabin. Sliced the sirloin into strips, diced the vegetables and threw them into a skillet simmering with butter. The ingredients hit with a sizzle, and when the meat was seared on the outside, he poured in a generous amount of the merlot, heating it on medium for about 15 minutes until it was a dense reduction.

Normally he would spend more time intentionally mixing up the way he cooked this dish, but being as hungry as he was, he stuck to the tried-and-true recipe he made once a week.

He opened up a few cabinet doors looking for plates and found a stack of aluminum dishes. Very fitting for log cabins; not suitable for Aiden's hipster taste. But he could care less at this point.

Aiden tried to occupy his thoughts with something productive as he ate, such as an itinerary for the next few days. But with each bite, he found himself feeling increasingly discontent, and the cabin grew smaller and smaller. Whispers of inadequacy kept creeping out of his subconscious.

"What am I doing here?" he thought.

He needed to get out.

He looked at his watch. 5:15. Still enough daylight for some escapism.

Aiden grabbed his brown hoodie, started up the car and drove south. He remembered Dad telling him that the further south, the more serene the imagery.

Not that he really cared about serenity right now. He just needed some air.

Although he hated the stereotype, Aiden did have a mental "nothing box" which let him drown out all his thoughts and focus on a sole action. In this case, that action was driving.

He continued along the main roads, using the sun as his compass. About 20 minutes later, the main county road came to a dead end. He spotted a small dirt road behind him through his side mirror. Feeling frustrated but not enough to be defeated, Aiden backed up, turned down the dirt road and pressed on.

The road was quite scenic and surrounded with dense trees. He drove up a small but steady incline, which then crested the top of the slope and came to an opening.

"Wow," he said out loud.

The southern-most tip of the island stretched out over steep cliffs with rich green grass growing along the field in front of the cliff. To Aiden, it felt much more like Ireland than the Pacific Northwest.

He stopped his car in a small turn-off lot. Thought twice, then locked his door anyway.

Aiden walked toward the cliff. A wide landscape

of grass preceded a steep drop down to the ocean. The waves were crashing up against the rocky cliffs, and the sun was beginning to set off in the distance. Arbutis leaves were scattered along the edge, crunching with each step he took.

He sat down on the rocky edge, closed his eyes and soaked it in. Suddenly, his worries and anxieties felt a little more distant.

He heard a different set of footsteps crunching in the background. He turned around and saw a woman approaching.

The grocery store cashier.

"Could this island be any smaller?" he grumbled to himself.

She was wearing baggy jeans, moccasins and a faded orange cardigan.

Mismatched.

Then again, this was Cielo.

Aiden was too far out in the open to sneak away unseen. He gave her a small nod of acknowledgement, hoping that she'd sense that he was occupied.

She didn't pick up on that. If she did, she clearly didn't care.

"First day here and you've already discovered a local secret," she said.

Locals seemed to know how to declare one's newness to the island with subtle yet blatant accusations of intrusion and ignorance. Aiden didn't know whether to smile at the notion or give her the finger.

"Sorry for tainting it with my presence," he responded. Even with his back to her, Aiden could tell she was looking at him with that soft gaze she held earlier at the store.

"Well that's the beauty of a rocky shoreline like Sunset Strip. The waves give it a proper cleanse every day from anything too foreign."

While it was an insult, Aiden picked up on the humor behind it. She may be overly vocal, but he couldn't deny that she had a decent sense of dry wit.

"You come here often?" he asked, still facing the setting sun.

"Try to; it's sort of a daily ritual of mine. Cashiers see a lot of people each day – even in a place as small as Cielo. Solitude does wonders for the soul, especially when the socializing wears one thin."

"I can understand that," Aiden said, his voice offering a slight jab at their interaction earlier.

"Sorry if I was a bit harsh today at the store," she said. "Cielo's known to be a friendly place; hope I didn't ruin that expectation for you."

"Well, you know what they say: every rose has its thorn," he said, followed by a subtle exhale through his nose. Sarcasm is great compensation for lacking confidence.

"Well played, sir," she said.

Aiden was still sitting facing the shore and she was still standing off to his right. It was time to surrender to courtesy.

"Aiden," he said, turning toward her and extending his hand. "Aiden Lawrence."

She met his gaze and slowly reached for his hand.

"Pleased to meet you, Aiden. Name's Rosemary. Rosemary Friesen."

"Nice to meet you as well, Rosemary."

Rosemary took a seat next to Aiden on the rocky shoreline.

"So tell me about yourself, Mr. Lawrence. You a city boy?"

City boy.

Aiden always had a problem with that label. There was a fine line between residing somewhere and claiming its culture as your own. And the hustle-and-bustle pace of city life lost its appeal in the last year or so. Especially when it came to crowded, claustrophobic public transit.

"Sure," he responded. "Live in the U-District of Seattle."

"You look a little old to be a student. How old are you? What are you studying?"

Prying already? Aiden knew he shouldn't be that surprised.

"Turning 30 this year," he said calmly. "Studying business, but taking some time off."

"Ah, 'reflecting,' right?" Rosemary said, surprisingly free of sarcasm.

"More or less. Just wasn't feeling it anymore. Working as a server at a downtown restaurant for the meantime."

"Interesting."

Aiden was confused by that comment, wondering whether to be flattered or uncomfortable.

"What makes you say that?"

As before, she held her gaze and almost seemed to take inventory with her eyes.

Strange enough, it didn't feel threatening.

"Life has a way of teaching you how to read people," she said. "Just at the surface initially."

They sat in silence for a minute, watching the sun approach the horizon.

"And what brings you here?" Rosemary asked.

"Just took an evening drive," Aiden said.

"I mean here," Rosemary said, her tone a bit heavier. "What brings an intelligent, big-city guy like you to Cielo Island of all places?"

Good question, Aiden thought. Throughout the process of making the necessary arrangements to get to the island, he didn't really get down to the "why" factor.

"Call it a transition period," he said.

"Fair enough," Rosemary agreed.

Aiden picked up the slightest hint of suspicion in her tone. Maybe not suspicion, but doubt nonetheless.

"Looking for a different answer?" he pressed.

"Look, Mr. Lawrence. I don't know you from Adam, and I'm not about to prod into your personal life the second you step foot on this rock. Maybe I don't even want to know," she said, after which she looked off to the setting sun. She held her silence, clearly planning how to articulate her thoughts as the waves continued to crash against the rocks below.

"People don't just stumble across this place. It isn't exactly the hottest tourist spot in the region, and yuppies don't come here to start their careers. People either grow up here, or they run here to escape from somewhere else."

Aiden didn't respond immediately. He didn't know if he should. Was Rosemary baiting him? Trying to lead him down a path to reach a conclusion?

He stood up, still facing southwest. He slowly stepped toward the edge to look down.

Big leap, he thought.

Big leaps require a significant amount of trust, and even more faith – neither of these things came easily to Aiden, especially when it came to people. Soured relationships didn't help, and he wasn't about to start spilling his guts to a complete stranger the first night on some remote island.

There was something about Rosemary, though. Like she cared about him. Almost a maternal aura.

"Things change," he finally said, not dropping his guard. "Life changes, people change. Yeah, I know there's always the next step, whatever. Sometimes I don't care about that next step. You just go with the flow."

"And this is where 'the flow' took you?" she asked, looking up at him.

"Maybe it did, maybe it didn't. I'm here now. What's next doesn't matter."

"Sounds like more of a cross road than a transition," she said.

"What's the difference?"

"Transitions have a clear 'next step.' You know where you're heading. There's fear, but there's certainty."

She turned to the right and pointed to the ground, using her finger to mark two spots in the dirt.

"Point A, Point B," she said, pointing to the two respective dots. "You have your time at Point A, and sooner or later you need to move to Point B. They're entirely different and a lot of change will be involved. But you at least have an idea of what's coming next."

Aiden nodded and bit the side of his lip. Rosemary clearly liked her own analogies, but she seemed to be going somewhere with this one, and she had his attention.

Philosophical discussions were fine by him because you can explore the abstract without bringing yourself into the picture. That's how he saw it, at least.

He preferred it that way.

As Aiden turned to face her, Rosemary dusted away the two dots and drew a cross in the dirt.

"A cross road is the end of something, at which point you're staring into the unknown. There are a lot of unmarked roads ahead of you, and you have no assurance as to what's down each road."

She let it hang in the silence for a bit. So did he. The sun was now touching the horizon, but neither of them seemed to notice.

"Maybe 'crossfire' is a better word," Aiden said. "More variables, more players, less safety."

As he spoke, Rosemary squinted her eyes and brought her brows closer together, as if to say "Ah ha!" in response to Aiden's words. As if he had somehow disclosed too much and let her in.

"So how do you move forward?" she asked. Aiden's defenses were alerted, and he swiftly segued back to the philosophical argument. Rosemary was no shrink, and this look-out point was no therapist couch.

"Why should you?" Aiden asked. "Why does it always have to be about moving forward? What's so wrong with the present?"

"The present isn't a bad place, Aiden. And moving forward doesn't always mean a change of scenery."

"Is standing still really so bad?" he asked.

Rosemary nodded, her eyes open and engaged. Not defensive, but caring. She really did seem to care. That maternal vibe again.

"The way I see it," she said, "when you come to a cross road – or crossfire, whatever you want to call it – you've got two options. You can stay put; don't proceed any further. You're in the safe zone. But you're not safe. You're held captive by fear. And this fear is, in all irony, far more dangerous than the crossfire itself. Yes, you're exposed to external dangers if you move forward – but fear paralyzes you."

Aiden wasn't expecting that strong of a response.

She paused, stood up and looked out as the sun was mostly set.

"In a sense, fear is pride inside out. 'What will happen to *me*?' 'What will they think of *me*?' 'Why should *I* be the one to make the first move?' You make yourself the victimized star of your own universe. And of course, your problems and anxieties are far more interesting than anyone else's."

Aiden stood there, looking at her. Dumbstruck. Never thought he'd hear such revelations from a cashier.

"By the way," Rosemary said, "when I say 'you,' it's entirely figurative. I know nothing about you other than your sense of style, and this is no attempt at trying to figure you out. I'm just an old lady who likes to ramble."

Aiden nodded in acknowledgement and approval. Silence seemed golden.

"There's a second option," Rosemary continued. "Take that next step. Walk into the crossfire. Yes, you'll feel terrified and you're positive that you're paralyzed by inadequacy. You're not. You'll take some hits, but you'll live. And when you take those first few steps and glance back at your foot prints, you'll see that you survived. You made progress. You're carving out a destiny for yourself. Fear will be replaced by astonishment."

Rosemary broke her gaze, looked at the darkening horizon and turned her head back toward Aiden. "You should head back," she said. "Gets dark quick here."

She stood up and started to walk back toward the gravel lot. Aiden was still trying to connect all the dots of her theory as he followed her to the cars.

"Wow," he finally said out loud. "When do you think these things up?"

Rosemary smiled a small smile.

"When you spend most of your time working behind a cash register, your mind tends to wander," she said. "You learn to read people. Most everyone walks around as an advertisement of themselves, in everything from their demeanor to their grocery lists."

They walked side by side toward the parked cars. Aiden had to chuckle out loud. "Not gonna lie, for all your talk about the beauty of life and such, that sounds like you're putting a blanket treatment on everyone when you don't know the first thing about them."

Rosemary opened her car door and paused before moving to the driver seat. "You're a lot more similar to the rest of us than you'd like to think."

5. LOST PERSONA

5:25 AM came far too early for Aiden.

It was a sleepless night for the most part. He tended to not sleep that well the first night in a new place – let alone a place as dark, cold and rustic as Dad's cabin.

Moonlight crept in through the living room windows, directly across from the loft. The light kept his senses alert and his mind racing. Not with anxiety; just restlessness.

He managed to sleep an hour here and there but the interruptions kept a deep sleep at bay. He heard frogs outside. Gusts of wind shook the trees, sending maple leaves and cedar bristles and small twigs onto the metal roof.

The distractions held little power compared to the white noise from today's conversation with Rosemary.

Or was it yesterday? Sleepless nights make it hard to keep track of time.

Either way, he wasn't expecting to get hit with such existential conversation when he got in his car that afternoon. Still, it was nice to at least have made some human contact. The talk was intellectually stimulating and he appreciated her thoughts – strange as the interaction was.

His mind switched back to assessing his current situation. The cabin was cold. Aiden guessed there wasn't much insulation. He wrapped himself in the two thin quilts he found on the loft bed. They weren't keeping him warm enough, and he was still wearing the t-shirt and sweatpants he changed into when he got back from yesterday's drive.

He climbed down the ladder and walked over to the wood stove. Couldn't remember the last time he made an actual fire. There were a few pieces of firewood in a small black bucket by the stove along with a box of matches.

But no paper.

He remembered having a copy of *The Seattle Times* in the Civic. He put on his hoodie and braved the harsh wind to fetch the paper from the passenger seat. Yesterday's news was today's fuel source. Once insightful, now dispensable.

Much of life seemed to share that fate.

He ran back into the house, slammed the door shut and quickly crumpled up the paper, stacked it in with the firewood and lit a match. Took a few attempts, but the flames roared to life.

Aiden climbed back up to the loft and crawled under the quilts, still wearing his hoodie. He clenched his left hand into a fist and used his other hand to warm it, then curled up and brought his legs close to his stomach, adopting the fetal position.

Aiden wasn't just cold; he was worn out and felt vulnerable to the cabin itself, like it was closing in on his lack of confidence and wealth of uncertainty.

Seemed to be the trend. Being without a sense of direction or even a roadmap made for an unfortunate transition.

The heat quickly filled the room and rose up to the loft. Too warm for the quilts.

Aiden threw them off and rolled over to his side and felt some fatigue kicking in.

But his mind still couldn't shut down. Still couldn't drown out the frogs and the wind.

Still couldn't answer Rosemary's question.

"What brings an intelligent, big-city guy like you to Cielo Island of all places?"

He didn't know.

It was getting warmer. He unzipped the hoodie and threw it to the far corner of the loft.

"Intelligent" was the last connotation he would assign to himself right now. He had no degree, no professional experience outside of food service, no romantic companions with which to find blissful distraction, no strong friendships to rely on for guidance and no healthy family relationships to turn to for support – emotional or financial.

That's how Aiden saw it, at least. The last thing he wanted to be was a pity-whore always finding something wrong with his situation. He knew he fell victim to that.

"Your problems and anxieties are far more interesting than anyone else's," Rosemary had said.

She had a point.

He still was too warm.

Stripped down to his grey t-shirt and black briefs. It was almost too warm for the shirt, but Aiden had always been self-conscious about his hairy gut, even when no one else was around.

Finally he was comfortable. He stretched out on his back and enjoyed the heat, hoping that it would relax his mind into a deep sleep.

Sleep didn't come, so he surrendered to restlessness.

Aiden sat up, swung his legs over to the side of the bed and looked down from the loft.

The moon lit up the cabin just enough to make it visible to the eye. It had an eerie ambiance, no doubt, but it also had a sense of comfort that Aiden couldn't deny.

Peaceful darkness.

Calming isolation.

Quiet.

He couldn't pin it down.

He didn't need to.

All he had to do was give up hopes of sleeping that night. But the cabin's eerie comfort was countered by trying to make sense of the vague memories of his last time on Cielo – memories conjured up by the cabin's furnishings.

Aiden got off the bed and climbed down the ladder, feeling a noticeable coolness compared to the warmth of the loft. The balance was good, so he left his pants off. It was dark enough that even he could barely see himself.

He stood near the fireplace with his back facing the heat, warming his bare legs while he looked outward into the moon-lit living room. A small love seat stood against the loft wall to his left and an arm chair was on the opposite wall. Where Dad must have read his books by the fire, he thought.

The cabin had a natural cooling effect – more psychological than physical. The sensation that comes when you're not sure what lies around the corner. Or even directly in front of you.

Aiden could see, but the sights were what brought the eerie coolness. Remnants of Dad. His passions, his hobbies. His life.

Dad's old fishing pole was mounted on the wall above the fireplace. He took Aiden to fish at a lake when they came to the island. A small, rain-fed lake that was a popular spot for swimming and fishing. The island council had to bring in a load of trout each year to replenish the fish supply.

On that summer day 17 years ago, Dad taught Aiden how to fish. He threw the line and handed the pole over to Aiden, who wasn't confident to do it himself. More than a dozen casts and not one bite – unless it was Dad who cast it. Even the trout sensed his lack of confidence and affirmed his absent desire for adventure.

The fishing pole and its respective experience should have brought a peaceful stillness to Aiden's spirit. Where he looks back and sees a definitive moment in his life. One of those "All is well" milestones.

Instead, it set the precedent for his self-assigned inferiority. Wherever there's inferiority, there's a dominating figure acting as the source of inferior energy. Dad just happened to be on the receiving end of it – not by Aiden's choice or by Dad's doing. Just circumstantial.

Why circumstances played out the way they did, Aiden didn't know. But he didn't try to change or counter them. In Rosemary's words, he let himself become the "victimized star" of his world. Everyone else was living in that world, always one step ahead of

Aiden.

His legs were getting warm. Time to move.

He sat in the nearby arm chair, its cool velvet upholstery refreshingly comfortable on his warm skin. There was a small end table on the right side. On it was a picture.

Aiden and Dad in downtown Seattle from two Christmases ago. Dad looked happily at Mom who was behind the camera. Aiden's face told the viewer that the yuletide greetings of Christmas were far from his mind. He wanted to be somewhere else.

This picture was on display at Dad's funeral.

It was the last picture of them together.

He was stuck with that dissatisfied expression for the rest of his life, and Dad went to the grave before another picture could be taken. Before Aiden could express any gratitude or appreciation. Mom was transferred to a nursing home shortly after.

That memory haunted Aiden every day since the funeral. The photo was the first thing he saw when he walked into the cabin but couldn't bear to acknowledge it for fear of having to relive the memory.

Fear of admitting to the rest of the story.

Aiden didn't cry at the funeral; he still hadn't cried. He was simply numb that day, and he remained numb to this day. He was still too numb to feel any remorse or closure.

Closure involves all the facts, and he knew which ones ought to remain off the record.

That was his life, his fate. He forged that fate for himself. And here he was, sitting in the chair where Dad must have read great stories, prayed for his family and reflected on a life well lived.

Aiden felt more distanced from human contact than ever. He sat there, motionless and still with quiet breaths.

"I don't know how to grieve."

He said it out loud and remained motionless, unsure how to physically respond to those words.

Those words were more revelatory than confessional. Maybe the most important revelation he'd ever had.

Maybe the *only* one he'd ever had.

Aiden was self-aware, no doubt. He lived his life in retrospect. When he did live in the present, it was purely analytical. Looking around and dissecting what he saw. People, things, smells, sounds.

He wasn't one to analyze himself.

Until now.

It was this cabin. He didn't have any specific memories of him and Dad here, but it was a reminder of the start of Aiden's self-destructive perception of himself and a cruel world revolving around him in mockery, scorn and judgment.

It still held that power over him. He always felt the lack of confidence, but never had it been so vivid as being in the cabin and practically feeling Dad's presence here. Aiden didn't believe in the supernatural, but he believed that memories could become imbedded in respective physical objects and can then be emanated back to their subjects. Like the fishing pole.

Maybe there was more about Dad to be learned from this place, from his belongings.

Maybe Aiden wanted to know more, to glean insights about the father he never took the time to get to know.

Or maybe, just maybe, cutting off his ties with the cabin and Cielo altogether was his way out.

Maybe it was the first step on his road to recovery.

His emotional emancipation after which he could experience human contact.

His liberation from self-doubt.

This was it. This was his beginning, the reason that brought him back to Cielo after all these years.

He was sure of it.

He felt sure.

Sure enough.

Aiden was going to sell the cabin.

6. MEMORY'S DOCK

Late September manifested itself along Canoe Drive. The pavement was covered with red leaves from the bordering maple trees. Countless trees extended their top branches far out over the middle of the road, providing a tunnel of shelter for cars and creatures alike.

Chickadees and gold thrushes sang their songs as they weaved in and out of the trees. Grey squirrels hopped across bridges made of branches, collecting seeds and nuts for a late breakfast. Few cars were on the road, and the deer seized the opportunity to cross to the other side of the woods.

There was a stillness in the air, a thin fog drifting below the forest canopy.

All Aiden cared about was the Americano he so desperately needed as he sped down the narrow road.

Last night's spurts of insomnia left him feeling like the undead: eyes dry, mouth parched, joints sore. Sleep is so crucial but is the first thing that's sacrificed to make room for living a lively existence.

Aiden was hardly thriving and would gladly give up any activity to catch up on sleep.

Partying wasn't the interference; his subconscious was. At 8:30 in the morning after minimal rest, a dose of straight caffeine would at least push him out of this walking slumber and exhaust the last of his energy so that he could sleep tonight.

He turned onto Borough Boulevard, driving for a few blocks with his eyes peeled for a coffee shop. Finally spotted a small burgundy cottage with a sign hanging from a trellis that read "The Bean House." He pulled into one of the three car slots in the gravel driveway.

The single-story cottage shared a plot of land with a large willow tree that stood just to the right of the building, its branches draping along the roof and shedding their yellow leaves onto the front steps and driveway.

The door revealed a quaint room. Dark brown trim accented the cream-colored wall.

The paint was chipped in places, giving the space a weathered look. A long bar ran against the back wall with five stools. Three tables between the bar and the front door.

Walls adorned with funky, Bohemian art.

Rosemary was sitting at the middle table by herself, holding a black ceramic mug and reading a newspaper.

She looked up.

"Doesn't get much smaller than this," Aiden thought to himself.

He actually was pleased to see her. Didn't consider her a friend by any means but she seemed well networked. A source for local information. Maybe she knew of a contractor he could hire to fix up the cabin.

"Good morning," he said with a dimple-inducing grin, hoping it looked sincere.

She nodded in return, with that same subtle smile.

"Mind helping me out?" he asked.

"I can later. My shift starts in 10 minutes."

Rosemary didn't want to talk?

"Meet me at the Harvest Cafe at noon and we can talk then, just a few blocks down," she said, standing up and walking toward the door.

Fair enough, he thought.

Aiden nodded in agreement, made a mental note of the time and place, then turned to the counter.

He ordered a large Americano and sat at her vacant seat, turning the paper back to its front page. *The Cielo Platform*. A weekly paper. Cielo must not have enough news for a daily.

He flipped to the classifieds, looking for names of contractors. Circled a few. But what good were names without references? He could wait till noon to ask Rosemary.

That was more than three hours to pass, and this was Cielo.

He downed the coffee in three gulps and felt the strong substance hit his stomach with an abrasive warmth.

Perfect balance.

Aiden rolled up the paper, paid his tab and hopped back in the car. No way would he spend three hours in the Borough.

* * *

The 15-minute drive back to the cabin put him just after 9 o'clock. He threw the keys on the loveseat and grabbed a change of clothes from his duffle bag. It was time to shower.

He walked into the small bathroom looking for a towel, seeing none. Didn't surprise him. He could always go back into town to buy one later. For the time being, he would just use a spare hoodie. Probably not even absorbent but he could make it work.

Aiden went to draw the curtains, then realized the cabin had no curtains. That didn't surprise him much either, so he brought the clean clothes in with him and closed the bathroom door. Public showers and locker rooms always made Aiden feel exposed, almost exploited; they're filled with guys who either parade around their sculpted physiques or are too comfortable with their countless curves and folds. Aiden saw himself in an imaginary line-up, naked, ranked based on levels of attractiveness – physical, emotional and social. In that spectrum, he placed himself on the low end.

Even when he was the only person within a mile – like today – he still didn't shower or undress completely unless he was securely blocked from all visibility.

Aiden turned off the lights. Even more privacy that way.

He hopped in the stall, closed the curtain, disrobed and then turned on the water.

To his great joy, there was a decent supply of hot water; Dad must have set up an automatic withdrawal with the power company and never cancelled the agreement. A thorough cleanse within the solitude of the shower rinsed away the residue of a sleepless night. He let the water run over his body – he didn't know how long, and didn't care.

He dried off with the hoodie and got dressed, taking his time. Then he turned the lights back on.

Still had time to kill. Not in the cabin.

Aiden grabbed his keys and wallet and hopped back into the Civic. He had a destination in mind. Not for the sake of reminiscing, just observation. To see what it looked like 17 years later.

He was going to find that lake.

* * *

After driving southwest for about 20 minutes, Aiden spotted an old wooden sign with the lake's name – Lake Providence – carved into it, standing in a parking lot composed of wood chips, sawdust and dirt. A narrow path led the way through the dense trees. Small maples, pines and cedars. The trees kept the lake from being visible from the road. He walked for almost a mile before coming to a clearing when he saw the lake.

It looked more like a pond now. Aiden was struck by how much smaller the world could seem through an adult's eye, stripped of childlike ignorance that perceives the physical surroundings as beautiful and grandiose. Blissful ignorance, to be sure.

The star-shaped body of water had several little coves, some with the water up the edge, others with a bit of shore. The lake's underside was layered with semi-jagged rocks – not sharp enough to cut through skin, just not too smooth. Aiden remembered Dad telling him how the stones were warmed by the sun and helped keep the lake at a moderate temperature. Who knew if it's true.

The path continued around the perimeter of the lake, bordered by the variety of trees.

The leaves had turned and were littering the water's surface, along with pollen and stray wood chips.

He looked down and picked up a small maple leaf. It was still a bit green at the center but was surrounded by a deep red that burned from the edges toward the middle. The steady photosynthesis from the summer was beginning to die down and the leaves themselves were dying. A death which would then give nutrition to the soil that was home to so many other plants, as well as the tree itself. Like the Phoenix. Dying to live again.

"*Seriously?*" he said out loud.

He couldn't bear the thought of the island's hippie rhetoric beginning to resonate with him.

He dropped the leaf and walked.

Aiden was expecting to be hit by guilt or nausea when he spotted the small dock where he and Dad fished from.

Neither emotion was there; this was good. Maybe the decision to sell the cabin ensured that the recurrence of guilt would not, in fact, recur.

He could live with that. Frankly, there wasn't much reason to stay there any longer. He told himself he simply wanted to see what the lake looked like now. His ulterior motive was to put guilt to the test, and he knew this. The jury that was his conscious had spoken, and he was free to leave.

Aiden looked at his watch. 11:38. The hours had already passed?

Time to meet Rosemary for lunch.

7. POINT OF REFERENCE

The Harvest Cafe occupied the right end of a strip mall filled with a realty office, a boutique store, an art gallery and a vacant space. Island economies depend on a heavy tourist season, and summer had seen a bit of a drop from previous years; the increase in ferry fares made traveling to Cielo a steep investment for a family. If the business didn't attract enough tourists, it depended on local patrons throughout the year. Without tourists, the fate of vacancy is inevitable.

This quaint restaurant appeared to be doing alright business-wise. Most of the dining area's 10 tables were filled and Aiden was happy to have found a two-person table by the window that looked out at the water. He took a swig of his red wine as he waited for Rosemary.

She walked through the door just after noon, spotted him and approached the table, draping her purse and maroon jacket around her chair before sitting down.

"Busy day at the store," she said, "I may just have an appetite now."

Aiden was ready to get the information he needed.

"I need to know —"

"Nope, order first," she said as a young waitress brought over two laminated, one-page menus. "What's the point of meeting for lunch if you do all the 'meeting' before lunch?"

He nodded.

"I'll have the cob salad, dressing on the side, please," she said to the waitress.

"I'll take the pesto chicken panini," Aiden said. Should go well with the wine.

The young girl nodded, jotted it down in her notepad and took away the menus.

"So, how was your first night on the island?"

It was as if she knew how to get under his skin, and that she was ready to pry.

Or she actually was interested in his well-being. Who knew.

"It was a night, and today is a new day," he replied, choosing his words carefully.

Offering too much insight could lead to another long conversation when all he really wanted was a referral.

"And how did it compare to the city?"

Either Rosemary was on to another interview, or she did in fact care about how his night went.

"Quieter. Much quieter."

After he responded, he clued in: Rosemary was a caring individual. Her maternal instincts made her content with her zero-respect job because, being the mother hen that she was, she got to check up on everyone.

A bit nosey, yes.

Maybe manipulative.

Sincere?

Absolutely.

Regardless, he could tell she valued reciprocity.

"And how was your night, Rosemary?" he asked.

Her lips slowly stretched into a genuine smile.

"See Aiden? It doesn't hurt to be a little courteous," she said without the slightest trace of scorn.

Had he heard those words from anyone else, he would've immediately hid behind pre-existing walls to protect himself from any impending attacks. From Rosemary, it almost felt nurturing. He looked out the window, exhaled from his nose and turned back to her. A slight grin acknowledged her words.

The waitress brought out their meals, and Rosemary closed her eyes momentarily. A short prayer, Aiden thought.

"Now, you said you wanted to ask me something," she said as she tossed the salad with her fork.

Aiden took a bite of his sandwich, swallowed and took another swig of the wine.

"I'm selling my cabin but it needs some repairs, so I'm looking for a reasonable but reliable contractor." He pulled the folded newspaper out of his pocket and put the classifieds in front of her.

"Recognize any of these names?"

She took a few bites, picked up the paper and searched the names.

"Chase Avery," she said.

"You know him?"

"He's done a lot of work around the island. Born and raised, keeps to himself. Definitely not the most social guy."

"Not important, I just need a job done well," Aiden said. "Sounds like he could be the one."

They both went back to their meals, enjoying the warm dining room as they looked out at the cold Fall day.

"Can I ask you something in return, Aiden?"

"Sure."

"Why are you selling the cabin?"

Aiden went on to explain that he would use the money to buy a place in Seattle, finish up school and move on.

"Move on from what?" she asked. "Is this your point-A-to-point-B plan?"

"Like you said, making a plan and moving forward," Aiden said, acknowledging yesterday's conversation. "It's gotta happen sometime, right?"

She held his gaze.

"Sounds a bit more like running away than moving forward."

Aiden felt his stomach contract. The way it did whenever he was questioned or suspected of withheld information, of hidden meaning.

When strangers got too close to him on a bus.

When Dad tried to teach him to fish.

Maternal instincts or not, Aiden was offended by Rosemary's allegation. She crossed the line and he wasn't about to keep quiet.

"Look, this is your turn to listen," he said, fists tightening and shoulders tensing. "I've known you for less than 24 hours, and one thing is clear: you look at people through a mother's perspective, looking for pieces that are missing or parts that are broken. You need to better these people, because it gives you the affirmation that you're contributing to making them a better person. Let me tell you something. You're not the only one who can read people."

He turned to the window, took a breath and looked back at her. She seemed unfazed; he kept going.

"You're ignorant and judgmental. You don't know the first thing about someone when you meet them. And while you may have genuine intentions, you're only lording yourself over everyone else."

The words spewed out of self-defense. Aiden was surprised by his own words, even though this was his natural reaction to criticism. He'd feel a surge of confidence, then immediate deflation. He had no control over these episodes, which were typically succeeded by withdrawal and regret, along with the hope that it at least accomplished something.

When he finally finished unloading, he stopped to look at her, expecting to see some sort of a breakthrough.

What he saw were those same maternal eyes and that same smile, almost as if she foresaw his reaction.

Aiden wasn't expecting that.

"All I'm doing is trying to get a better idea of why you're so ready to get rid of this cabin," she finally said. "If you want a quick sale, I'd recommend one guy. If you're looking to bring out the best in the cabin and attract a responsible buyer, I'd recommend another."

She took a sip of her water, placed the glass on the table and folded her hands in her lap. "Context is everything, Aiden."

Aiden felt spent. He saw that his words had no effect, as he wished they had. He turned to the window again.

"If it's about the money, why not just rent out the place?" she asked. "You'd have a steady income and could support yourself on the mainland and still have the cabin available for an island retreat when you need it."

"It's not about the money," Aiden said. Still couldn't make eye contact. "I'm trying to let go."

"Of what?"

His eyes were wide but they weren't focusing on anything. When he did notice his hollow stare reflecting in the window, he saw his own ugliness. He refocused his thoughts.

"Of being tied down to something that doesn't even exist." He'd let down his guard, and knew that she would pry at it now. No turning back.

He told Rosemary that the cabin wasn't just a bag of money waiting to be handed over to him, but that it was holding him back from living the life he wanted.

Aiden could hardly believe that he was opening up at all, but he hadn't put up his defenses in time, and he hadn't the strength to keep fighting back.

"I'm resentful, and I hate that. I'm willing to change and I'm willing to learn, but I can't do that with this baggage."

Rosemary looked down, nodded a couple times, then raised her eyes back to Aiden's.

"I know you don't want to hear any advice right now, especially from an old bag like me. But I think the bigger question is what you're running toward, not from."

He was confused, and his furrowed eyebrows showed it.

"If isolating yourself from this baggage is what you want," she said, "then having an outcome of isolating yourself may be the problem. And in my honest opinion, you strike me as an isolated person. Seclusion seems to be your only friend."

He didn't fight it. He just let her finish, because arguing got him nowhere with this woman.

"I'm a person of faith, but I'm not afraid to look at truths found in other belief systems," she said. "Taoism always resonated with me. The more we can let go of what we long for, what we love, the more real and present our love is able to become. Giving up your quest for isolation may in fact bring you a bit more inner peace. An appetite for community."

She let the words settle before pressing on.

"What do you love, Aiden? What do you need?"

He sat still, looking out the window.

"They say that the greatest human need is to be known. If selling the cabin will help you get to know yourself more, you should do it. But I'd at least give yourself a couple months before you make a decision."

The waitress came over to clear their plates. They were the only ones in the restaurant, so they saw no need to open up the table for other customers.

"You mentioned business school," she said, changing gears completely. "What made you interested in that?"

Aiden blinked a few times and answered while looking outside.

"No particular reason, no family ties. Dad was a construction worker and a handy-man, always fixing things around the house; he built the cabin. I was so determined to do something different. Business school meant moving out and moving up. Heading to the city to become successful."

In all honesty, he didn't know what "successful" meant.

"Here's the last bit of advice I'll give you, Aiden, at least for today," Rosemary said with a smirk. "Wait a few months. You're tattered, and that's okay. But just wait a bit. You see a little clearer from up high."

She put $30 on the table. "I should get back to work. Call Chase Avery. He'll give you a quote for the job."

Aiden had no words to say. He finally nodded in acknowledgment. He couldn't do much else.

8. EXPOSURE

The fridge was empty.

Aiden had kept his distance from human contact since his lunch with Rosemary, making all of his meals at the cabin.

He got creative. He had to. There's only so much one can make using rice, salt and pepper.

He drove to the grocery store to get some substance. Even two chicken breasts would do the trick.

He just had to make it through the doors, past the checkout counter and back to the car. Back to the safety of the cabin.

Safety?

Aiden hardly considered the cabin a haven, but at least it offered quiet comfort. He steered the Civic into the store's parking lot and turned off the engine, taking a deep breath through his nose and exhaling from his mouth. Opened the car door, closed it and locked it.

He walked through the store's double-door entrance, noticed that Rosemary wasn't working at the till today. A teenage girl was be covering her shift.

Strolled past the produce section toward the deli. Surveyed the meat selection. A decent variety of pork and beef cuts.

He glanced to the left. Chicken breasts, legs, wings and thighs. All fresh, nothing frozen; saran-wrapped Styrofoam containers with two or three pieces of meat. He grabbed a two-pack of breasts.

"Almost out of here," he thought.

Aiden walked to the checkout counter, chicken in his left hand. He placed the meat on the conveyer belt and pulled his wallet from his back pocket. The teen employee scanned the meat.

"$4.27," she said.

Aiden handed her a $5 bill; she gave him the change along with a white plastic bag holding the chicken.

He walked toward the door, looking down as he tried to stuff the coins into the pocket of his jeans.

He felt a sharp pain pierce his left side as his shirt tore.

He cussed, stopped and turned to the left. His shirt had caught on a metal coat rack displaying Cielo-themed shirts.

Felt his side.

Blood.

Just a surface cut, but his shirt was completely torn. He looked around. At least eight locals stopped and stared at him. Aiden felt his face turn white, the blood draining from his head. He felt faint. Weak.

Exposed.

He turned to the store's entrance and ran past the doors, fumbling to find his keys once he got to the car.

Opened the door.

Threw the chicken in the car.

Hopped in the driver's seat and slammed the door shut.

Started the engine.

Sped out of the parking lot.

Fled from the scene.

He gripped the wheel. His breathing didn't slow.

He wasn't hungry anymore.

9. ASSESSED VALUE

Aiden's second week on Cielo started with a call from Chase Avery, giving a date he could do the initial assessment. Chase was finishing up a big renovation job down at Slumber Valley, a ritzy community on the south end of the island.

Aiden spent the days reading, walking and cooking but not enjoying any of it.

Not wanting to waste any more time, Aiden booked it for the following day. Chase asked for a couple hours to scan over the place and made it clear that any questions should be saved until after the assessment was completed.

Understandable.

Today, Chase wore fitted jeans, a long-sleeve grey t-shirt and black boots; cleaner than one might expect a contractor to look, but Chase's sturdy physique made him look more rugged than stylish.

Chase tested, pulled, pushed and examined all corners of the property thoroughly, making notes on a small pad as he made his way through the cabin while Aiden struggled to reconcile why Chase looked strangely familiar.

His cold demeanor wasn't inviting when he arrived that morning, so Aiden chose to pass the time apart from Chase's company by driving around.

When he returned an hour later, the hired hand was standing in the gravel driveway, facing the cabin, his strong legs spread just beyond shoulder width. He was looking at the notepad.

"What's the damage?" Aiden asked as he slowly walked up the driveway toward Chase.

"Needs a new roof," he said, not turning to acknowledge Aiden's presence. "Shingles will do the trick. Deck has been hacked by termites. Supporting beam on the front porch should be replaced, and the 2x4s are on their way out. I give it another year till the deck collapses. Interior needs some work too."

Aiden worked to absorb the information. He mentally prepared himself for a high bill and was willing to invest so he could walk away with a nice profit and a clean slate.

"And what's this going to cost me?"

"Just shy of eighteen grand."

Aiden exhaled a profanity without noticing. He expected to pay a sum for this project. Eighteen grand was a different matter. He didn't consider himself a cheapskate but knew himself to be wary of large monetary investments – or any kind of investment, for that matter.

All he had to do now was face the current situation. Chase was known to be the best when it came to local carpenters and Aiden needed to secure the job in order to permanently distance himself from Cielo.

"Whatever it takes," he finally mustered as he looked toward the cabin.

"Takes to what?" Chase asked.

"To sell it," Aiden responded.

"Then you'd better get on it," Chase said. "Repairs should be made soon. Won't ruin the cabin's structure if you don't, but your chances of selling this place as is are slim — at least for a decent price."

"Decent is do-able," Aiden said. "Think this could be done in a month's time?"

"Doubt it. I'm a one-man show, so it takes time but I work quick and I'm the best around here. Can't begin without knowing what you want, so we'd better head over to Sandman Island tomorrow morning to look at the hardware store. Better selection than here. We can work within your budget but I need to know what you want to work towards. 8 o'clock."

"That early?"

"You want this done soon, right?"

"That's true," Aiden said. "Where do I meet you?"

"Ferry landing."

Any amount of progress would further bridge the gap until departure time, Aiden thought.

"I'll see you soon," he said.

10. SHAME

Aiden jolted out of his sleep when he heard the thunder.

It was dark. His arms were stiff, his vision blurry. Ears were fully functioning as he took in the crashing sounds coming from outside the cabin. Violent winds blew small branches onto the roof. Rain pounded against the windows.

He looked at the clock. 4:48 in the morning. He tried to get comfortable in bed.

He wasn't comfortable.

Closed his eyes. The noise reminded him of Seattle. Different circumstances but similar volumes, especially when cop cars or ambulances would race down the street outside his apartment.

He felt his neck start to relax; slowly, his eyes grew heavy.

Crash.

All his muscles were shocked to life with the sound of glass breaking in the living room.

He jumped out of bed and climbed down the ladder, wearing a T-shirt and sweatpants.

His eyes swept across the room, seeing shards of glass scattered on the wood floor and a large branch protruding into the cabin where the window used to be.

Gusts of wind blew the rain through the new hole into the living room. Aiden knew he had to act fast, but he had no idea what to do.

The hole in the wall needed to be covered up.

Quickly.

More and more rain blew into the house.

He needed to find a board. Had to be somewhere on the property.

He ran toward the door to put on his shoes when a piercing pain shot into his right foot.

He screamed, stopped, raised his foot and brought it behind him, grabbing it with his right hand. He turned to see what it was.

Glass.

He knew he should have looked before running around.

He pulled out the glass. Winced. Threw it to the side.

Aiden hobbled over to the entrance, shoved his feet into his shoes and opened the door. He grabbed a flashlight off the counter top.

The wind and rain immediately blasted his face. He ran down the stairs and went behind the house, desperately looking for some scrap wood. Small branches and debris covered the dirt, each footstep making a squishing sound.

He found two pieces of plywood leaning against the backside of the house.

He grabbed one piece of soaked wood and hauled it back into the cabin, shutting the door behind him.

Aiden knew he would need nails if these boards were going to block out the wind and keep the heat inside.

"Where would Dad keep nails?"

He propped the wood against the kitchen counter and began opening every drawer he saw.

None in the kitchen.

He moved to the desk drawers.

His right foot burned with pain.

No nails in the desk either.

He ran to the bathroom. Found an old shoe box. Opened it, finding a couple dozen or so nails and screws. He grabbed all the nails and put them in his pant pocket.

But there was no hammer.

He needed something. Anything that could pound a nail.

Thunder resounded throughout the cabin. Aiden flinched.

He ran back to the living room and faced the broken window. Maybe there was a rock right outside?

He opened the door again and ran out, fortunately finding two large rocks at the bottom of a deck post.

He only needed one.

Grabbed it and ran back inside. His foot continued to sting. He pressed through the pain.

Aiden set the rock down and kicked the broken glass aside with his right foot, putting all of his weight on his left side.

He grabbed the plywood and placed it over the broken window. Pressed against it with his left forearm. Used his other hand to reach into his pocket and pull out a nail. Placed it in his left hand and held it in the upper-left corner. He then grabbed the rock with his right hand, centered it over the nail's head, slowly brought it back toward his face and used all his strength to pound the nail.

It sunk the nail into the board with one movement.

Aiden grinned.

He positioned himself against the board to repeat this on the upper-right corner.

The rock slid off the nail's head and crushed his right pinky against the board.

Aiden screamed, cursed and dropped the rock. He backed away and clasped his hands together, hunched over in pain. The board swung down and was hanging by the left corner. A strong gust blew against the board, sending it to the ground with a crash.

Aiden felt his stomach sink.

He needed to get the wall secure, but he didn't know how to.

The wind kept blowing rain onto his face.

His foot ached.

His finger throbbed.

He grabbed the board and held it against the hole with both arms.

He didn't know what else to do.

He dropped down on his knees.

He felt helpless.

Defenseless.

Alone.

Lost.

He slammed his head against the board's surface.

Dad would have known what to do.

Chase could have secured the board in an instant.

Aiden's knees ached.

His clothes dripped.
His arms locked.
His foot bled.
His right pinky nail turned black.
He closed his eyes.
All he felt was shame.

11. DECISION POINTS

Aiden parked the Civic along the road just up from the landing, locking the driver's door.

Chase was waiting down at the terminal; his truck was nowhere to be seen.

"Who's driving?" Aiden asked.

"No one. It's free to walk on."

"Aren't we going over to buy materials?"

"Shop now, buy later," Chase answered, almost hitting Aiden with his broad shoulders as he walked by.

More islander insider knowledge, Aiden assumed. If it saved him money, so be it.

The small ferry had already pulled into the dock. Two cars drove off onto Cielo.

They walked along the right side of the ramp designated for foot passengers and made their way up the boat's stairs.

"See you in a half hour," Chase said as he opened the door to the passenger area. The man didn't want company, and Aiden wasn't going to pursue it.

The interior of the boat looked just like the ferry Aiden set foot on a couple weeks ago. So much that he chose to go straight to the outside deck and bypass any fellow travelers.

He pushed the doors open as the boat pulled out of the Cielo dock and he felt the familiar gust of salt water wind blasting his face, stinging his eyes at first contact.

He winced and turned his head away from the breeze, opening them slowly to let them adjust.

The early afternoon sun broke through the clouds and brightly reflected off the ocean, as if someone had opened a jar of gold glitter and dumped it over the water. It was mesmerizing, but focusing on it strained the eyes.

Aiden always thought beauty was overrated. The glittery sea was no exception.

Yet he kept staring, emptying his thoughts out into the wind and freeing his mind of any kind of work.

For a few moments free of interruption.

It was quiet.

Peaceful.

He coughed quickly when the cigarette smoke blew his way.

Aiden turned to the right and saw Chase leaning against the deck rail, cigarette in hand.

So much for peace.

The crashing waves were joined by the growls coming from Aiden's stomach. He had forgotten to eat before leaving the cabin.

He did recall seeing a dining galley in the main passenger area. Inside he went.

The small food station had a sparse selection. A few hot dogs stuck on a rotating heating device; four burgers wrapped up in aluminum foil, probably sitting for at least an hour.

Alas, something familiar: Ivar's clam chowder. Probably below the standards of the Seattle location, but Aiden was relieved to see something he recognized.

He gave the cashier a $5 bill in exchange for a small container and ate the soup quickly.

The half-hour ride was over before he knew it. Aiden looked out the window and saw a small harbor crowded with boats and docks, leading up to a slew of buildings along the water line.

He wiped his mouth with a paper napkin, threw the container away and walked down to the car deck where Chase was waiting.

"Where we headed?" he asked.

"Hartman's Hardware," Chase said. "About 10 minutes up the main drag."

They walked off the boat along with a handful of other passengers and turned on to Front Street, past several restaurants, bars, gift shops and info centers. This town felt busier than the Borough.

Neither spoke.

"You come here often?" Aiden finally asked, hoping to break the awkward silence.

"Only for work," Chase said. "Can't stand it over here. Bunch of hicks."

"Not your type?"

"People aren't my type," he said. "Cielo at least gives you anonymity."

Aiden didn't care to push the banter into a conversation.

He was relieved to see a large grey barn with a billboard hanging above the double-door entrance which read "Hartman's Hardware."

Time to shop.

"I'll show you what you can afford," Chase said, pulling a small notepad out of his pocket. "Based on the estimate and my rates, this place will give you the most bang for your buck."

He walked ahead of Aiden toward the lumber section. "A cedar porch will suit the cabin's style. That's your best bet for the deck materials. I can put on an inexpensive finish that'll add some visual value."

Aiden didn't know what else to do but nod.

Chase led him to the interior details department, starting with a stainless steel sink followed by granite counter tops.

Aiden was happy with the products' appearance and could see them both implemented in the cabin, bringing out a rustic, tasteful ambiance.

He agreed on the suggestions and Chase took note of it.

"If you're re-doing the deck, roof and kitchen, you may as well put in a proper floor. A floating wood floor isn't totally secured but it's glued down and there's some cushion below it, and it looks as good as the real deal. I factored it into the quote already."

Aiden didn't know whether to give a stamp of approval or just to nod in case Chase had already put in the order for the materials.

"Sure," he finally said.

"That covers it," Chase said, walking past Aiden toward the counter. "I'll go put in the order."

"I need a window," Aiden said.

Chase turned around.

"Where?"

"The main window in the living room. Storm took it out last night."

He left it at that.

"Sure," Chase said. "That's easy."

Ten minutes later, Chase returned and walked past Aiden toward the front door.

"Are we done here?" Aiden sheepishly inquired.

"Do what you want with your time," he said, pulling out a cigarette and lighting up as soon as he stepped out of the store. "I'm off the clock now."

Aiden could see what Rosemary meant when she referred to Chase as an all-business kind of guy.

Not wanting to lose face, Aiden maintained professional rapport.

"So you'll start working tomorrow?"

"Not till Tuesday," Chase said, maintaining eye contact and exhaling a drag from his nostrils and the side of his mouth. "The owner of the other house I'm working on needed me to take today off, which is why I'm talking to you right now. That job will be done Monday, so you'll see me after that."

And with that, Chase was off.

Not knowing what to do, Aiden walked back into the store and looked around for about 15 minutes. Quickly bored, he asked an employee if he knew anything about the ferry schedule. Aiden learned that the boats ran on the hour – in this case, the next one left in five minutes.

Aiden ran down Front Street, hoping against hope that he'd make it in time. Just as he turned the corner, he saw the small boat pulling out of the dock.

Chase was barely visible as he leaned on the deck rail, looking at the harbor as the ferry moved further away.

An hour wait it was, on another God-forsaken rock. His left foot started to sting again.

Aiden bought a copy of *The Seattle Times* and sat bitterly in the ferry terminal, cursing under his breath.

"Thanks for the heads-up, bastard."

12. MOCKINGBIRD

Aiden hated cleaning up messes – especially ones that weren't his fault.

He stepped outside the cabin's front door to survey the damage wreaked by the recent windstorm.

Broken branches. Scattered pine cones. Smeared dirt.

Shattered glass.

He'd seen it all yesterday morning on the way to the ferry. He just didn't care to acknowledge it then.

He grumbled as he stepped onto the deck, his canvas shoes squishing against the damp maple leaves. His socks immediately became wet.

He grunted.

He was too frustrated yesterday at having to wait so long in the ferry terminal and he had no interest in cleaning up the property when he got back to the cabin. He had known Chase for a mere 24 hours and was already pissed at him. The local could've at least given him a heads-up about the ferry schedule. But no, Aiden thought, that would be too much free-of-charge work.

Aiden could still hear the unspoken insults shouted from Chase's strong figure, reaffirming Aiden's own short-comings.

The debris reminded him of his failure to fix a simple problem.

He leaned down and picked up the large branch from the deck, dragging it down the stairs to the right side of the driveway. He dropped it there.

Aiden heard a screeching sound from behind.

Turned. Saw nothing.

Another screech.

Tilted his head up. Saw a crow perched on the cabin's broken gutter, staring down at him.

Aiden ignored the bird and bent over to pick up a few more branches, dragging each one next to the large limb.

Soon enough, a pile had formed. Aiden didn't get every single branch, but he had cleaned up enough. He thought of burning the pile. Getting rid of the mess.

He'd bury the ashes later.

The crow screeched again.

Aiden flinched. Regained his focus.

He walked back to the cabin door, glancing up at the crow. It kept staring.

Aiden marched past the crow and, once inside, opened the cabinet below the kitchen sink, looking for lighter fluid. Found it sitting next to a box of matches. He grabbed both and walked back outside to the pile.

Each step made a squishing sound.

He grunted again.

Standing over the pile, he twisted the cap off the fluid bottle and squeezed, drenching the already wet branches with a heavy dose of the chemical.

Set the bottle down. Opened the box of matches. Struck one.

The match stick broke.

He threw it in the pile.

Grabbed another. It broke too.

Grabbed a third match. Didn't break, but wouldn't ignite. Probably wet from the sink, he thought.

Aiden grabbed another.

Another.

Another.

None would ignite.

He looked at the pile. Blood pounded through his temples.

Forehead perspired.

Jaw tightened.

Aiden felt nothing but failure and frustration.

The crow screeched again.

Aiden went rigid, but only momentarily. He grabbed a fuel-soaked branch, turned around and hurled it toward the bird.

He missed, hitting the roof. The bird continued to scream at him.

Aiden stared at it, his eyes wide with exhaustion. Shoulders tense. Legs heavy.

The crow flew away. Aiden was left with a pile of failure in the driveway.

He went back into the cabin and locked the door for rest of the day.

13. MARKETS, FREEDOMS

Nothing screams "last resort" like frozen pizza.

Aiden was still reeling at the cost of the cabin's renovation. But it was a necessary sacrifice, one that would put a permanent barrier between himself and Cielo.

Unfortunately, he had to endure another weekend before Chase could start working.

So he turned to cooking, exploring all corners of the culinary world as an escape. The past week filled the cabin with flavors and aromas spanning from Latin America and Southeast Asia to Eastern Europe and small town America – occasionally resulting in victories.

The French recipes took a turn for the worse. Extreme precision requires utmost dedication, and Aiden's reservoir of patience was running dry. He spent an entire day seeking to master an authentic Hollandaise but kept botching it.

Hour after hour of attempting to add egg yolks to hot butter without it curdling.

Trip after trip to the store for replacement eggs.

Trash bag after trash bag of curdled yoke.

Hence, the pizza.

Yet in all truth, this disc of obesity would hit the spot today. Aiden set the hot pan on the stovetop, letting the cheese settle before cutting it.

Lying on the counter next to the stove was a paperback copy of F. Scott Fitzgerald's *This Side Of Paradise*, which he re-read the past week during the hours he wasn't cooking. In his third read of the book, Aiden still found himself perplexed by the characters – mainly Amory Blaine, the leading man. Amory, in a sense, had become his friend. He was Aiden's only friend, actually. Someone who did in fact experience the seasons of life. Who took the great journey of becoming human, and who arrived in due time.

Yet for this, Aiden resented Amory. Never wishing ill on him, but envying his arrival.

Amory thrived at Princeton.

Aiden couldn't last at a state university.

Amory found love.

Aiden ran from human relationships.

Amory had the world in his hand.

Aiden had frozen pizza.

He grabbed the old copy of *The Cielo Platform* from his book bag and turned to the back page, glancing at the community calendar. Searching for something to do. He needed to get out of the cabin, to get some fresh air. Some sense of living.

He saw that there was Saturday Farmer's Market in the Borough. Given that this was one of the few days the sun made itself visible since his time on Cielo, Aiden seized the opportunity. He crammed down a few more slices of pizza, wrapped the remaining pieces in tin foil and tossed them in the fridge.

* * *

15 minutes later Aiden pulled on to Borough Boulevard, looking for parking along the already-filled side streets. He finally found a spot, locked the car and crossed the main drag over to a large field where the market was set up.

The sun was shining down on the dozen or so booths and tents occupied by islanders of all ages.

Young kids – probably 8 years old – selling plastic bags of popcorn for a dollar.

An elderly woman displaying her driftwood photo frames bordered with sea glass.

A teenage girl creating immaculate henna designs on a customer's forearm.

Several artists and photographers selling their exquisite – and expensive – paintings and photos.

A truck bed filled with lettuce, potatoes, apples and beets, all locally grown. At least that's what the sign said.

Aiden wondered how these people actually made enough livelihood off these sales.

Especially the high-priced items.

He wasn't sold on much, so he kept strolling.

At least he could kill time. Anything to distance himself from the smell of botched Hollandaise.

After circling the perimeter, he turned toward a small bend with three booths in it: one with a massage chair, one with a jewelry display, one with an assortment of cooking spices.

Cooking.

Finally something that caught his interest.

He casually walked over to the spice booth, which was run by a man that Aiden could only assume was a stereotypical stoner islander, and offered him a courteous head nod.

The guy, probably in his early 30s, sported a faded red bandana wrapped around shaggy brown locks which hanged down to his shoulders and a grey vest, unbuttoned with no shirt underneath, along with Bermuda shorts and bare feet.

Looked strong as a horse.

Taking "laid back" to a new level, Aiden thought to himself.

"You name it, I got it," the vendor said with casual confidence.

Aiden had to chuckle. Island folk sure think highly of themselves.

"And Cielo, of all places, has any spice variety I might need?" he asked, skeptical eyebrows raised.

"Well, you obviously haven't met Onyx yet," he said, arms spread, head tilted back and thumbs pointing at himself.

Onyx? Onyx? This hippie took pride being named after a rock?

"Apparently I haven't," Aiden said.

He brushed aside the subtle arrogance and leaned over the wood table that supported an array of aromas. Ten bowls, each with a spice mixture representing cuisines from various regions.

"What can I do ya for today?" Onyx asked.

Aiden was actually impressed with the variety of spices, especially for a place like Cielo.

Countless scents, all extraordinary – apart from Onyx's slight body odor.

"You make these?" Aiden asked.

"Yeah man, all here on the rock. Grow what I can,

then order what I can't. But it's all in the mixing process – that's where the magic happens."

Aiden wondered what else he was growing.

"Can I ask you something?"

"Shoot away, man" Onyx said.

"These vendors – is this all they do? Like, is this the only work they can find here?"

"Far from it dude. See those paintings over there?" He pointed toward an elderly woman under a white tent. "She's the math teacher up at the school. She's old, man, been teaching since before the Flood. But her painting keeps her going."

Onyx turned to the left and nodded toward a middle-aged couple, both wearing denim overalls. "Them there, she's an accountant and he's a lawyer. Their work can get so dry though, so they started up a huge garden on their property and then sell whatever they don't eat. This here at the market, this is closeted talent's coming-out party."

The topic got Aiden's business mindset going.

"So this is your side job?" he asked.

"No way, this is it for me."

"You sell enough product to make a living? What's your ROI like?"

"Well I'm a simple man, bro. Live in a small yurt, no indoor plumbing – but who really needs that, right? Got a big rain-catch tank out back that I use for cooking and drinking, a wood stove and a small shack out back over a hole in the ground. No better way to connect a man to his primitive nature. That's how I like it, anyhoo."

Aiden didn't even know how to respond – or whether to at all.

"How do you shower?" he asked – then realized that personal hygiene probably isn't Onyx's highest priority.

"Does it look like that's much of an issue for me?"

Before Aiden could articulate a response, Onyx continued.

"Nine months out of the year I head down to Surprise Cove, ditch all my clothes and take a plunge – almost every day. Yeah it's cold and does a number on your manhood at first, but I'll take salt water over a hot shower any day. A neighbor puts me up in their shower for the other three months. Nothing's as freeing or refreshing as being so connected with the world around you, shedding all human convention and getting back to the way we're supposed to be living."

"And that is?"

"Wild and free, man," he said, maintaining eye contact with Aiden. "Wild and free."

Aiden was taken back by Onyx's candidness – he could barely stomach the thought of public showers, let alone skinny dipping at a public beach.

"And you never worry about someone showing up? Or a group of kids running by?"

"Dude, anything goes here, and that's why guys like me are still around," Onyx said. "You should give it a try, might loosen you up a bit."

What was with this constant prodding of having to "loosen up" or change his ways? These islanders seem so bent on singling out mainlanders.

"Well you're not the first to suggest loosening up – just took it to a different level," Aiden shot back.

Yet he couldn't help but smile. This guy had no inhibitions, and seemed perfectly happy with that. For the first time, the hippie Bohemian lifestyle seemed to make some sense to Aiden.

Onyx smiled back.

"So tell me about these spices. What would you recommend?"

"Totally depends on your taste. I supply most of the restaurants on the rock with their spices, and they use them for whatever theme they're promoting on their menus. You cook much?"

"Cooking's pretty much all I do right now," Aiden answered.

Onyx nodded a few times and looked down at the different bowls, as if he were a doctor prescribing medicine to a sick patient, his locks bobbing along with his head.

"You like seafood?"

"If the occasion calls for it."

"Gotcha," he said as he picked up a bowl and lifted it to Aiden's face.

"Try this one. Pacific Fusion."

Aiden took a sniff and immediately noticed the variety of scents that worked together to make a fresh earthy flavor.

"Basil, thyme, rosemary and lemon zest, threw in with a bit of cumin, paprika and black pepper," Onyx explained. "Rub it on a slab of halibut and top it with some onion and a few cloves of garlic and you're set."

"Squeezed lemon to finish it off?" Aiden suggested.

"Wouldn't be complete without it, brotha!"

This guy knows his stuff.

"How much do I owe you?"

"$4 for a sachet of it."

Not bad.

He handed Onyx a $5 bill.

"Keep the change. Consider it payment for your expertise."

"Will do, good sir. Take it easy and hit me up if you want some other ideas for the cooking."

Aiden dipped his head to say good-bye and turned to go back to the car.

To his surprise, the small dose of human interaction lifted his spirits. A friendly hippie had broken Aiden's preconceptions of island folk.

What he needed now was halibut.

He drove over to the store, grabbed a couple fillets and hit the check-out line.

No surprise that Rosemary was working today.

He had dreaded the thought of seeing her again after she shot down his pretenses at their lunch meeting.

Today, he felt at ease.

Almost calm.

He even initiated the conversation this time.

"Well if it ain't Lady Wisdom," he said with a smile.

She displayed her warm demeanor as always.

"Nice to see you, Mr. Lawrence. It's been awhile. What have you been up to?"

"Waiting for Chase to call back, cooking up a storm and reading."

"Reading?"

"*This Side Of Paradise*, just finished it yesterday – for the third time, actually. You read it?"

"Nope, just heard a lot about it," she said.

"Why don't I lend it to you? I've got it in my car. Wouldn't mind hearing your thoughts on it."

Rosemary dipped her head, raising her eyebrows at him.

"Wouldn't mind hearing my thoughts? Do my ears deceive me?" she said with a chuckle.

"Nope, you're hearing it right. I'll go grab it and bring it over."

"That would be nice – so would some money for the groceries, of course."

"Right," he said, grabbing cash from his wallet.

He ran back to the car, grabbed the book and returned to give it to Rosemary. The conversation that awaited could go any direction, he realized.

Now time to whip up some dinner. It was a fairly successful day on the town, and he left with a new bout of motivation for cooking. Along with an appetite.

Onyx's words repeated in his head as he drove back to the cabin.

"Wild and free, man. Wild and free."

14. OLD SOULS SPEAK

Sunday. Just two days away from the start of demolition and reconstruction. And how slowly the hours crept by.

To distract himself, he took on the challenge of making an authentic boeuf bourguignon, mastered by French chefs and made accessible by Julia Child. And with a start-to-finish time of nearly 4 hours, it helped carve away another day on the rock.

Aiden set aside an entire Sunday afternoon for the task. Any other day would find Chase hammering away on the deck or scraping old shingles off the rood. French cooking couldn't be interrupted by such distractions. Partly because the intricate measurements demanded the utmost precision; mainly because the ingredients cost an arm and a leg to purchase. With the $1,000 deposit he gave Chase last week, this wasn't a recipe he could afford to botch over and over like the Hollandaise.

Standing at the small counter next to a window from which the afternoon sun peered in, he began the process.

Simmer four thick strips of bacon in boiling water for 10 minutes and then sear the bacon in butter, a base with which to sauté the beef cuts, carrots and sliced onions.

Combine the ingredients in a large casserole dish, sprinkle with flour and place in the oven pre-heated at 450. Remove after eight minutes, stir, re-sprinkle and re-heat for another eight minutes.

Add several cups of beef stock and full-bodied red wine, along with sautéed mushrooms and braised pearl onions with an herb bouquet of thyme, rosemary, basil and fennel.

Reduce oven to 350.

Hide away in the oven for three hours.

Prepare pasta over which to serve the stew.

Anticipate the finished dish.

Aiden enjoyed idle waiting as much as he loved public transit.. He threw on a hoodie, grabbed his keys and headed for the Civic in hopes of catching the sunset on the south end of the island.

He started up the car, letting the fluids circulate through the engine for a minute before shifting into first gear. He drove down Scarlet Lane and hung a left onto Canoe Drive.

Windows down, heat on high.

15 minutes later, he arrived at Sunset Strip. He frequented this locale every so often after lunch on weekdays. Most islanders were usually busy with work or occupied by household responsibilities, leaving him alone with the vast ocean view from the steep cliffs.

Whether reading a book or taking a stroll, Aiden usually experienced a heightened sense of isolation here. Not the oppressive loneliness he felt in the evenings at the cabin; rather the notion that he was the one man left in the world – a nurturing sentiment of solitude.

He had no such luck walking the strip this afternoon. Faces were scattered here and there, but the wide landside allowed visitors to settle apart from each other; visible, but not audible. At least not above the waves crashing against the cliff's rocky shore.

Aiden was comforted by that segregation.

Until he saw someone he recognized: Rosemary Friesen.

Initial eye-contact made conversation inevitable, so he caved and walked over to say hello.

She sat on the edge of a thicket of tall grasses. Dressed surprisingly chic with dark khakis, brown pumps and a black winter jacket. Her brown hair was up in a bun that hung just over the maroon scarf wrapped around her neck. A gold watch on her wrist.

He saw she was holding his copy of *This Side Of Paradise*, with her index finger holding her place near the half-way mark.

"I see you made a dent in it," Aiden said, head dipping down to the book.

She smiled back, lifting it up while holding eye contact.

"I actually was thinking of you today," she said.

He couldn't help but chuckle.

"Ah yes, here we go again."

He walked to her side and sat down in the grass, one leg extended and the other bent with the knee cap up, providing a rest for his elbow. Surprised that the grass was dry enough to sit on comfortably.

They both looked out at the water, sitting quietly as the wind blew.

He turned to face her.

"And I suppose you want to know what I've been up to lately?" Aiden asked, taking note of their last talk.

"Of course," she said, nodding her head. "Of course."

He told her about the renovation process so far. The exchange was civil, unlike their previous banter. They were acquainted, had established a history of sorts and spoke as peers rather than strangers.

"Is the job finished yet?" she asked.

"Far from it, but Chase seems to know his stuff. We had the loveliest chat though. He's quite charming." Aiden cocked his head slightly so as to make eye contact with his eyebrows raised.

Rosemary gently smiled and closed her eyes. "That nephew of mine never did soften up much."

"Hold up – nephew?!" he asked alarmingly. The thought of Chase and Rosemary sharing a bloodline was preposterous.

She nodded as if there was nothing unusual about the connection she just mentioned. "You're saying that little miss optimism comes from the same heritage as Chase?" he asked.

"Aiden," she said, turning her face to his, "do you mean to tell me you're taken by surprise when families lack cohesion and commonality?"

Aiden knew he couldn't argue with that. He and Dad shared little apart from their genetic makeup, quite similar to Chase and Rosemary.

"Anyways," he said after the brief silence, "it needs a new roof and a new deck among other things. Not too cheap, that's for sure."

"There's a reason he charges top dollar," she said. "He's harsh and expensive, but efficient."

They both let the words settle before moving on.

"So the two of you are blood related?" Aiden asked.

"Through marriage," Rosemary said. "At least we were once."

"Did his parents split up?"

"Parents died a long time ago. His father was my husband's brother."

Aiden blinked, held his eyes shut, then opened them wide, staring her in the eye.

"You mean to tell me that after all this time and all these conversations, you've somehow forgotten to mention that you're married?" Aiden accused. "Why haven't I seen him around? Or even heard of him?"

Rosemary looked out at the coast, eyes narrowing on the horizon.

"Great question," she finally said, a slight mist covering her eyes. She adjusted her gold watch. "I've spent years asking that question."

Aiden knew he'd jumped to conclusions and falsely assumed she was happily married.

He struggled to form a question that would respect the issue's apparent sensitivity.

"Did he pass away?" he finally asked.

"I honestly don't know. But I have no right to be concerned."

She paused but held her gaze.

"We met in college. He was in pre-med and I was studying English literature. A friend set us up, and we fell for each other quite quickly – married six months later. We were naive, Aiden. We loved each other dearly, but our paths began to lead in different directions. I settled down and was content teaching high school English; his ambitions led him to further education, which I supported. But as the years passed, so did our connection. He went on to greener pastures, and brought the student intern along with him."

Aiden was shocked by the level of disclosure.

"I needed to get away from the familiarity of the city," she continued, "so I moved here. I went through my stages of denial, grief, anger and acceptance. But honestly, my failed marriage led me somewhere that I needed to be."

"And where was that?" he asked, at first unsure if he should but decided to based on their rapport.

"Being comfortable in my own skin."

She let the words linger.

"I spent years blaming myself for what happened, and I was exhausted. Guilt is pure poison."

Aiden looked away.

He swallowed.

"You can only stand on the edge of yourself for so long, Aiden."

She tucked a strand of loose hair behind her left ear.

Neither spoke for several moments. With Rosemary sitting next to him rather than across, Aiden saw them as two sojourners on a similar road. Both searching for answers. For healing.

"So, you were thinking of me today?" he asked with a smile. "And what might that be regarding?"

"This book," she said, holding it in her hand. "This Amory Blaine. I see a bit of myself in him – a bit of everyone in him. Countless people pass by me every day at the grocery store, many unaware of my own story and I of theirs."

She fanned through the book with her thumb, gazing down as if expecting the text to physically manifest itself and leap forth from the pages.

"Amory passes through a lot in this story," she noted, "and it accumulates into something at the end."

"I always viewed him as my antithesis," Aiden said.

"Too optimistic?" Rosemary asked. "Too successful?"

Her cutting analysis resonated with truth, and although it wasn't necessarily revelatory, Aiden agreed. He had initially brought up the correlation, so no offense could be taken.

He shook his head.

"What's wrong?" she asked.

"I'm sorry, but I have to be straight with you."

"Yes?"

Aiden looked her in the eye.

"What's your deal?" he asked.

"I beg your pardon?"

"You're a store cashier. You handle people's transactions. You stand in the same place every single day. What keeps you so insightful and optimistic when – no offense – your job is so monotonous?"

She raised her eyes as if she were reciting lines from a school play. Took a deep breath, held it in for a few seconds, then exhaled.

Aiden looked at her.

"Well?" he asked.

"That's it."

He furrowed his eyebrows.

"What's it?"

"Breathe in, breathe out," she said. "I know can't control everything, so I do what I can and I let God take care of the rest."

"And that keeps you happy?"

"I choose to smile," she said.

Aiden laughed.

"Oh Rosemary, such a simple life you live."

"You'd be surprised how far a little optimism can carry you in life, Aiden. It's my lifeline. You see the same people every day, but each person is in a different phase. Sometimes they're happy, sometimes they're not. Some days they're bubbling with passion and excitement, some days they seem almost dead with complacency."

"That's to be commended," he said. "I couldn't handle being around people that much. Let alone the same bunch of people."

"May seem boring, but it's an art. For just a few moments, in that small window of time while the customer's at the counter buying what have you, you have the chance to speak into their lives – even if you don't speak at all."

They sat in silence.

The wind continued to blow through the tall grass, creating a loud whistle – as if passing along secrets from person to person.

"Would you like to come for dinner?" he asked suddenly but sincerely, almost surprised that he had initiated a social invitation.

Rosemary's expression showed she was surprised by the offer – as was Aiden.

"I've got boeuf bourguignon in the oven and it's far more than I would eat on my own," he said. "What do you say?"

Her appreciation was evident and her demeanor eager.

"I would be honored," she finally responded. "Fine cooking has never been my forté, so making dinner is one less thing I'd have to do tonight."

So they drove to the cabin, Rosemary riding with

Aiden since she had walked today.

They continued their earlier conversation about literature during the drive.

Upon arrival, she sat the table as he took the food out of the oven and placed it on the top of the stove. They continued talking as he brought out the tin plates, steel cutlery and wine glasses; still had enough wine for them each to have some. He was fascinated by Rosemary's experience in the classroom setting, almost inspiring him to someday go back to school.

With the first bite, Aiden experienced flavors like never before. The tenderness of the beef, the sweetness in the onions, the warmth of the wine, the accents of the thyme, basil and pepper.

For Aiden, it was the family gathering he never experienced growing up. Family meals were often accompanied by feelings of inferiority, ungratefulness and imprisonment. At least that's how he had felt, overdramatizing as he often did.

None of those sentiments were present at the cabin that evening. Aiden felt safe in the company of Rosemary – a woman with a marred past who made no pretense of perfection. Such transparency felt so foreign.

He knew this meal wasn't just food for his sustenance. This was life. The cabin no longer felt like a prison; today, it was their cathedral – their haven. A Eucharist with no officiant or priest. For the first time, Aiden felt as though he belonged. Enjoying provisions and celebrating unity between two broken people.

He wanted more.

He craved community.

He craved the thought of being known.

But there was no confessional booth at this Eucharist. He kept his cravings at bay, along with the secret he carried for so long.

It's the one thing he did well.

15. THE EXCHANGE

With far too much ruckus going on to be able to enjoy reading inside, Aiden opened the cabin's front door and, to his pleasant surprise, the deck had already been torn down since he went inside an hour prior. All that remained between the front door and rocky soil was one cinder block stacked atop another operating as a temporary set of stairs.

Today, Chase wore a dirt-stained white tank top, understandable given the moderate temperature mixed with intensive labor. His biceps contracted as he lifted the old lumber to a pile just to the left of the cabin.

No grunts or heaves from Chase, just strength and stamina.

Aiden embarrassingly recalled his own loud grunts when lifting dish trays at the restaurant in Seattle. He'd now think twice before future complaints of physical strain after seeing Chase move so effortlessly between the cabin and the lumber pile.

Aiden observed Chase's frame, intimidated by his solidarity.

The sight of the demolished deck excited Aiden. Progress. As if threads that tied him to Cielo were unraveling. Yet that thrill was laced with subtle sentiments, not of loss, rather an indication that the end of his time on the island was in sight. All things – good and bad – come to an end sometime.

He stepped down using the cinder blocks and walked toward the pile, hands in his hoodie pockets.

"You move quick," he said, looking down at the moldy 2x4s.

"That a problem?" Chase asked. His deep, gravely voice made the question sound curt and short.

"Far from it," Aiden responded. "Your rates are high but I'm happy to invest in efficiency."

"What's the rush on selling this place, anyway?" Chase asked, continuing to stack the old lumber. "The housing market on Cielo got pulled down with the rest of the country's, and it's far from its prime right now. Your safest bet would be to fix it up as planned, sit on it for a few years with regular maintenance and then try again when the economy kicks up. You're gonna to lose if you sell now."

Contractor turned realtor. Aiden knew Chase charged a high dollar for his services – rightly so – but he didn't hire him as a financial advisor.

"Appreciate the advice, and in a perfect world that could work for me," Aiden retorted. "But I'm not losing anything 'cause I inherited it from my Dad. Just tying up loose ends."

Chase huffed out a laugh. "Loose ends?"

"Bloody hell!" Aiden exclaimed as his hands tightened into fists, clamming up out of defense. "Why does every person on this rock feel the need to press a visitor for every detail?"

A small smirk formed on Chase's strong jaw. "You're a little paranoid, that's all."

Aiden suddenly recalled where he had seen Chase before. The first day he arrived on the island and pulled up to the store. *"Fearful mainlanders always lock their cars and look over their shoulders,"* he had said. *"They've got a stressed-out mentality when they come here."*

He re-gained his composure. He didn't want to give Chase the satisfaction of letting him know he had pushed Aiden's limits.

"Paranoid or not, all I'm doing is dealing with and moving past a non-existent relationship. My Dad and I weren't close, I'm past that whole teen-angst phase. Cielo holds no significance to me. Fixing up the cabin and selling it are my priorities."

There, he said it. Simple enough.

"Cashing out," Chase said, pulling a measuring tape out of his tool belt and stretching it across the deck's longest side. "Nothing more to it than that."

Aiden didn't know what Chase meant. He waited for an explanation. Chase recorded the deck's dimensions in his note pad and moved to the adjacent supporting beams. "Milking what you can from this place, pissing on it and moving on. No harm in that, none at all."

Aiden couldn't decipher whether Chase was speaking through sarcasm, satire or sincerity.

Did it matter?

"I'm not pissing on anything," Aiden said. "What's it to you, anyways? You always talk smack to your clients? Not exactly what I'd call a healthy business model."

"No smack," Chase said. "Just calling it like I see it."

"Seems to be the norm around here. So how do you see it, then?"

"Life is one long exchange: cash out and move on," Chase said, measuring the height difference between the ground and the top of the stairs leading to the front door. "If this place is all you got, you're clearly only concerned with cashing out on this cabin to help ease your conscience. Everyone does it, so don't think you're an exception."

The words came rapidly, taking Aiden completely by surprise. He wasn't offended but not sure whether or not he should be. He more so wanted to know what Chase was getting at. Rosemary said he wasn't the friendliest guy; Aiden had assumed that to be synonymous with "quiet."

"And this philosophy has been going well for you?"

"Gets me my bottom line."

"Which is?"

"Me. You talk about selling the cabin to let you move on and live your life. Maybe even invite someone significant into your life, right?"

Chase's question hung in the air as he packed up his tools into a dirty canvas bag and threw them in the back of his pick-up.

Aiden could tell Chase was trying to bait him, but didn't know which direction to turn.

"Sure," he finally surrendered after several seconds. "I guess."

"Please," Chase said, rolling his eyes as he leaned against his truck with his arms crossed. "Monogamous relationships are just another thing to check off as part of the 'get everything' agenda – say what you want about how people bring out the best in you, 'cause you're only doing it for the security and property. I've got my own property – me."

Aiden couldn't believe how twisted – and existential – the assessment had become. But he wasn't leaving the argument without pushing back.

"So you're saying there's no real end other than getting whatever you can?" he asked.

"In all areas. I put bread on my table and clothes on my back – taking them off is someone else's delight. There's a flock of women on Cielo looking for nothing more than a hook-up, and I'm thrilled to help out any given day."

The air seemed to be sucked out of the quarter-acre plot.

Aiden had thought optimistic people like Rosemary and Onyx were the norm around here.

"Seems a little far-fetched," Aiden said. "You call this place Cielo – literally translated to 'heaven.' It's full of happy tree-huggers. I think you're speaking for yourself. Names mean something."

"Names don't mean shit," Chase retorted without missing a beat. "This island always gets talked about as the region's 'heaven.' There's as much cynicism and fatalism here as any inner city ghetto."

The curve balls kept coming. Aiden's neck perspired more and more as he realized the nihilistic worldview contained within Chase's overbearing strength.

"No offense," Aiden said, "but you have way too much time on your hands to think this deeply about modern man's condition."

"Man has no condition other than breaking down. People articulate the world however they want to. I don't bother 'cause there's nothing new under the sun.

Everything has been here since the start – nothing novice about it."

Aiden worked to wrap his mind around Chase's words. It wasn't as if a bleak outlook was foreign to him; Aiden was a self-proclaimed cynic conditioned by years of perceived rejection and failure that blew away any childhood ignorance. Chase, on the other hand, seemed bred to think this way. Aiden hated his cynicism; Chase secured his strength in his.

"If today is all that matters and if nothing new can be created," Aiden asked, "why would you waste your precious 'now' building homes? You're building. You're creating something that never existed before. Not too consistent with your talk."

"Construction is recycling," Chase said. "Seeds to trees, trees to lumber, lumber to houses, houses to burn piles, burn piles to ash. Life is just one big exchange leading toward entropy. You and me, we're breaking down right now."

With that, he hopped into the driver's seat of his truck, revved the loud engine and rolled down the window.

"Be back by 9 tomorrow morning with the lumber," he said. "Should have the stairs done by day's end."

It was as if the conversation never took place, Aiden thought. Chase didn't show the slightest hint of annoyance, turmoil or awkwardness that Aiden felt brewing inside.

What was this place, and why was Aiden here?

16. WHISPERS FROM PARCHMENTS PAST

As much as he'd like to forget it, Aiden continued mulling over Chase's unexpected manifesto over the following days, in the same way he recalled Rosemary's words at the Harvest Cafe. Aiden noticed a distinction: Chase's nihilistic outlook came out in a rapid-fire pace, strong enough to shake the foundation of his own worldview; Rosemary's sincere maternal words pierced like a needle and lingered like a tetanus shot.

Maybe he wasn't as intimidated by Chase's strong appearance as he thought he would be.

Maybe he was comforted by the fact that his own outlook wasn't the bleakest.

Maybe he was just overwhelmed by the price of the cabin's renovation.

Nonetheless, the cost was a necessary evil with a worthwhile end: a swift house sale and a one-way departure from Cielo.

The end would be worth it, but the cost still stung.

Still, Aiden felt peace, to some extent. Chase continued to work away at the cabin and Aiden explored the island's scenic roads.

As each day passed, the cabin progressed. The roof was nearly finished, dramatically reducing the noise levels during the day.

All was going along schedule until Chase was taken captive by the stomach flu earlier in the week. He had caught the bug and was out of commission for several days. While it put the work on hold, the end still was near, And Aiden knew he needed to start the inevitable process of sorting through and packing up Dad's possessions.

Most of it was to be boxed up and taken to Mom's place. Whatever wouldn't fit in a U-Haul truck, Aiden would pack into his own car.

That meeting would be one that has been in the works for almost three years. He saw Mom at the funeral and checked in on her shortly after, but they never did have much to talk about. Aiden hated making conversation and felt awkward offering condolences – even to his own mother.

He started cleaning the surface clutter in the living area; filtering out the small objects would leave fewer things to box up at the end.

Envelopes and stationary lay scattered across the surface of Dad's desk, one of the dozen or so pieces of furniture in the cabin. Most of the paper was unused, some had scribbles, some were tattered.

To the fire with the damaged goods, he decided.

Piece by piece he tossed the paper into the fireplace, saving anything that might be of interest to Mom. He set those things in a separate pile.

Then he came across a sealed envelope with an inscription that caught his eye.

His name and address.

Perplexed, he set the rest of the paper pieces on

the love seat and sat down in the chair next to the fire. Tore the envelope's seal with his index finger, damaging the envelope in the process. But who cared about envelopes; they were merely carriers meant to be discarded at once in favor of the piece of paper contained within.

Two pieces, in this case.

He carefully unfolded the tri-fold letters, which he quickly noticed were filled with beautiful calligraphy.

Only three words caught his attention. Three words that screamed above all the others.

"My dearest Aiden."

This was addressed to him? Written from the cabin? From whom?

From Dad.

A date was etched in the upper right corner: January 8, 2009.

Less than a month before Dad died.

Dad had come to the cabin? Aiden couldn't for the life of him recall Dad ever mentioning this trip. Just two weeks after their last Christmas together – when that haunting photo was taken.

Had he come for a mere vacation?

To get away from the city?

To seek God's guidance?

To write this letter?

Aiden sat in the chair and looked back to those first words.

"My dearest Aiden,

"I write this to you from Cielo, just after a less than jovial Christmas. You clearly were beside yourself, as you always seem to be. It saddens me to see a young man so bright, so full of endless potential, to see him so void of joy."

He stopped.

A thousand thoughts flew through his head like a photo reel. Aiden wasn't the only one who felt the sting of the dead relationship. Dad felt this pain, and was hurt by it as well.

Maybe even more than Aiden.

He must have intended to put this in the mail for Aiden to read.

Or did he?

He turned back to the pages, his stomach tightening.

"I've observed from a distance as your passion seems to have perished. That your sense of direction is lacking. It burdens a father to see his son so displeased with life.

"Let me make one thing clear before I continue. You are not a failure, Aiden. I have not nor will I ever take you to be one. The Lawrence family prevails. We always have, always will.

"But it starts with re-claiming our sense of awe.

"We're surrounded every day by beautiful imagery; distinct characteristics; stunning visuals. All of these provide great inspiration for living and creating. So why is it that in the span of a single hour, that inspiration can completely diminish?

"This back-and-forth pendulum with inspiration is a complex one, Aiden. Routine can be lethal to inspiration, but it can also birth a burning desire to break out, get away and create something beautiful. Or leave you stagnant without an ounce of creativity.

"Then there is stress. Be it financial, emotional or spiritual, stress puts all the focus on your problems. You will look down, not up. Not only will this strain your neck, but it will harden your heart.

"Often times, the most therapeutic thing is to get out of the office, away from technology and take a stroll through nature. But don't just stroll. Look up! Take in the mountains, the cloud

formations, the tree leaves whistling in the wind, the grey sky reflecting on the water.

"These are beautiful things that have been created.

"They're pure. They're right.

"They're true.

"The same is true with what we can create as human beings. When a thought is going through our minds, we can analyze it to death to try and make sense of it. Or, we can take it for what it is, regurgitate it and form it into something new. It may seem completely detached from reality, but as we pour ourselves into it and let it reflect an honest truth about ourselves, it becomes true to others as well.

"This isn't to be taken as a campaign for relative truth, Aiden. This a quest for universal truth. Truth that resonates with the heart of humanity. We are all part of a long-standing narrative. Don't venture down the path of relativity, as it will isolate you and leave you longing for an absolute. Truth that is revealed in a created work is not a new truth. It's a fresh lens placed on pre-existing truth.

"When you take a look at a metropolitan city and all of its progress, it's easy to assume that it has generated countless amounts of energy, electricity and materials. That decades ago, this city was merely a plot of land. Something entirely new must have been created, you think. Oh, if only it were true! Under the laws of physics, matter can never be created or destroyed – it can only be transferred. The amount of energy in our present day and age has not changed. It has merely been taken, transformed and retold.

"In many ways, this is how intellectual truth works. The truth has been there since the Garden of Eden. Through the ages, it has been harvested, sewn and re-harvested – sometimes for good, sometimes for bad, sometimes for pure evil. But the truth has prevailed nonetheless, and it's ours to find again.

"So this is our mandate: to search for those universal truths, and to tell them as only we can. People may hold the same system of truth and values, but no lens is the same.

"In this cycle of taking and re-telling, we find pieces of ourselves in people's truths.

"I trust that this letter has taken you by surprise, Aiden. And believe me, I know how you feel about receiving advice from anyone, let alone an old man like me. But these words have been on my heart for some time now, so better to place them on paper and send them on their way than let them remain dormant and unused.

"I know we have had our ups and downs, and I know you feel our relationship has withered. Why, I do not know. I may never know. But please know this: that your happiness will bring me great joy, whether I am a part of this happiness or not.

"And so I write this in hopes that you will see past the fog. That you will rediscover that sense of awe.

"I pray, son, that you will reclaim your right to greatness. That you will excel at that which you choose to pursue. But above all, I pray that you find your lens with which to tell the truth as only you can.

"I built this cabin for our family. For a center of memories. For the cultivation of creativity. For a retreat from the rest of the world and its worries. For helping each of us to become human. Promise me that you will take the time to invest in your own life by seeking sanctuary on Cielo sometime, Aiden. It's here for your wanting.

"You know where the key is.

"With fullest devotion, Dad."

17. CONFESSIONS AFTER MIDNIGHT

Rain pounded down on the Honda Civic's thin roof at a thundering pace. The engine and headlights were off as Aiden sat parked in the driveway.

Not his driveway.

He had driven here once and vaguely remembered the directions. Perhaps the only memory he had at this point that didn't plague him with guilt.

Aiden had been parked here for an hour or so. Why he ended up here at such a late hour – closing in on 1 o'clock in the morning – he honestly didn't know.

All he knew was that his heart hadn't stopped pounding since finding Dad's letter. Each sentence seemed to have sped up the blood flowing through his veins.

But he was cold. Rigid.

Hollow.

Those words read like a father's prayer for his son. A son who had done nothing but disrespect and alienate his father for decades.

Would things have turned out differently had Aiden received the letter in the mail prior to Dad's death?

Maybe.

Maybe he would have swallowed his pride.

Maybe he could have admitted his role in suffocating their relationship from the start.

But what was the use? Dad was dead.

His words weren't, and Aiden was paralyzed by them. Now with Dad's caring words and dying plea seared into Aiden's memory, the burden was too much to carry.

He needed somewhere to turn to.

Someone.

Someone higher than himself.

Dad was gone, and Aiden was beyond God's grace; he didn't even know if he believed in grace.

But he needed something. He needed to be known.

So he came to the only person who seemed remotely invested in his well-being.

Aiden got out of the car, walked to the porch and rang the doorbell. Knocked as well.

Nothing.

He knocked again. Louder.

Footsteps sounded from within, getting louder as the person walked to the door.

The door opened. Rosemary stood on the other side.

* * *

For an entire minute, her eyes locked with his as he stood there. Her expression showed that she didn't know why he was here; he didn't know how to form his words.

Yet her sympathetic eyes filled the silence, making him feel safe. He needed to feel safe.

Rosemary backed away and opened the door to let him in. Aiden walked across the hardwood floor into the living room, lit by a lamp and modestly decorated with antique furniture and a few wall paintings.

They both sat on the worn leather couch, sitting in silence. After several moments, he pulled the papers out of his hoodie pocket, handing them to Rosemary. She calmly opened it, carefully pulled out the folded pages and extended the folds. Tilted it toward the roaring fireplace for light. Folded it back up and handed it to him several minutes later.

The silence continued.

Aiden stood and walked over to the window, his face expressionless and his eyes hollow. Nothing was visible beyond the window pane but it made no difference.

He knew his true reflection.

"I killed him," he finally said.

His chest sunk and his shoulders dropped.

Rosemary said nothing, just remained on the couch.

He closed his eyes, then opened them again. His body was stiff.

"Almost two years ago, January. In Seattle. I was halfway through my sophomore year. School sucked. I lost my focus, had no clue where I would go with my degree or why I was even trying to get one."

The rain hadn't let up and its continuous impact with the ground rang through the windows.

He ran his left hand through his hair.

"I started drinking. Heavily. Alcohol was the only thing that distracted me from my loss of direction. Tried to prove myself as a man by how many shots I could take. And it always worked. Until it wore off and the hangovers kicked in the next morning."

He turned from the window and walked over to the fireplace, hands on the wooden mantel.

"I drove to a house party one night. Thought I could handle myself. Didn't work out that way. I needed control, to be tough. Nine shots of tequila later, I was gone."

Rosemary remained silent and motionless. She sat with her hands clasped in her lap, and her eyes never left Aiden's, even though he wasn't looking at her.

"I needed a ride home. I was a mess and wasn't going to stay there. Everyone was smashed and no one could drive. So I called Dad. Woke him up, demanded a ride home. He said it was too late, told me to catch a bus. I hate the bus, always did. I wouldn't do it."

He stood in silence, eyes wincing but remaining dry.

"I told him I hated him, that he was a lousy father. That if he cared about me, he'd come get me. So he did."

He sat down on the couch, legs spread wide as he leaned his hands on his thighs, lowering his head down.

"He told Mom he had to run an errand, that she didn't need to worry. He didn't have the heart to crush her with the news that her only child was piss drunk and needed daddy to come pick him up. So I waited, and I waited. He never came; I passed out at the party."

The silence hung, and Aiden grew increasingly tense.

"I woke up late the next morning, looked at my phone. Over 20 missed calls, all from home. I called Mom. Her voice was shaking."

Aiden's voice began to break.

"She said Dad went out for an errand in the middle of the night, and another car lost control on I-5. Driver fell asleep at the wheel, swerved into Dad's lane and hit his car. They both crashed into the median. Other guy was fine."

He stopped, tightened his jaw and squeezed his eyes shut.

"Dad died on impact."

Aiden slowly began to shake. His voice followed suit.

"If I had listened to him, he'd be alive and he'd have mailed me that stupid letter. If I had an ounce of self-respect, I wouldn't have gotten so trashed. He'd be here. Every time I see a bus or taxi or even a ferry, that phone conversation plays over in my head. And I hear myself demanding him to come. To drive to his death."

They sat in silence. At long last, Rosemary lifted a hand and placed it on his hand.

"She doesn't know," he said quietly. "My mom, I mean. She can't. No one does."

Rosemary said nothing.

The rain continued the pour outside.

"I don't want to come clean with her, so I don't talk to her anymore. She thinks I'm numb from not having a father anymore. She can't know it's 'cause I never was a son to him. That I killed him."

He pulled his hand away from Rosemary and stood up.

"She's in a nursing home. Did I tell you that?"

He looked her in the eye, and he knew she felt his pain. She said nothing and everything at once. It took all of his strength to make himself known; now he was empty. He couldn't bare any more of his soul tonight.

Aiden walked to the door and left.

18. PROVIDENCE REALIZED

Aiden stood on the small dock at Lake Providence, the rain drenching him from head to toe. His clothes weighed heavily. His heart felt stretched. His arms felt heavy. Yet he felt nothing.

The trees were stripped of their leaves, leaves that meshed with the wet soil and standing water. Dark clouds migrated across the sky, shifting with the strong winds that carried the rain across top of the lake.

How had he ended up here, on this island? Each passing day he felt increasingly exposed. Weak.

Overtaken by resentment, cowardice, anger and desperation.

He stood on the dock, overwhelmed, believing he had ruined himself by admitting fault.

Never in his life had Aiden made himself vulnerable; he didn't know how. He went through life clothed in anger and apathy.

Aiden grew up hating his own body. His entire image. Believed himself to be unattractive and unlovable in every way.

He was an unhinged man at war with self. A war that was awakening his senses for the first time.

He had lived as a question without answers, yet his encounters with Rosemary and Onyx – even with Chase – had pointed him toward something.

Somewhere.

In being exposed, in bearing his soul and becoming vulnerable to the rebuke of another, he no longer felt the presence of fear.

Telling Rosemary was the first step out of his self-imposed prison.

Dad's truth screamed at Aiden through that letter.

This morning, he wasn't in hiding. He had brought light to the darkness.

The morning light was becoming visible. He looked at his watch. 6:27 am.

Here he stood, drenched to the bone. Standing in the very place where he first resented his father. Where he first gave a voice to his own self-condemnation.

That condemnation was gone, put to rest by his confession.

He had shed that skin.

He was being washed clean.

His mind turned back to Onyx, the free-spirited hippie.

What was it he said?

"Shedding all human convention and getting back to the way we're supposed to be living. Wild and free, man. Wild and free."

Aiden didn't feel wild, but he desperately wanted to be free.

He wanted to feel both.

He needed to. To throw the lies and the masks aside, the pride and self-hatred that weighed him down.

To wash away the years wasted standing on the edge of himself, refusing to accept his brokenness.

The weight was heavy.

His clothes were heavy, too. Cold.

He unzipped his hoodie and threw it on the dock. It landed with a thud. Aiden felt a weight lift.

The relief spread throughout his body, every limb lifting from the ground in a brief surge of euphoria.

He wanted more. He needed more.

He pulled off his t-shirt, soaked to his skin and difficult to remove.

Exposing his skin to the wind and rain caused his heart to beat faster. Cold air danced across his upper body. He felt the endorphins flow through his veins.

For once, he felt aware.

Kicked off his shoes; his socks came off with the same movement.

He started to turn his head to look around, to see if anyone was near.

But he stopped himself from looking. He had just made his past known to Rosemary; he hardly cared if he was seen by passers-by.

Instead, he closed his eyes and breathed.

Deeply.

Aiden unbuckled his belt and pulled down his jeans and briefs, casting them to the side.

There he stood, naked for the world to see. Anyone could see the body he had learned to hate. His physical imperfection and emotional weakness were exposed to his surroundings. To the lake. To that ever-present voice of condemnation.

It was the most primitive Aiden had ever felt. Wild. Almost free.

Dad's words echoed in his mind.

"This a quest for universal truth. Truth that resonates at the heart of humanity. We are all part of a long-standing narrative."

The cold rain continued to fall on him; his eyes followed the water as it ran down his legs.

"Look up!" Dad had written.

Aiden tilted his head back. Arms extended, mouth open, catching the rain. Closed his eyes.

He thirsted, and he drank.

Then he cried out, unleashing a guttural howl from the depths of his being. Exorcising the demons that plagued him with guilt and disbelief.

His fists tightened. His cries grew louder and louder.

Until the tears weakened his voice. Along with his legs.

Aiden collapsed to his knees and his forehead smacked on the dock. Tears of grief, grief he had repressed for years. The sobs grew as he poured out the agony withheld from denying his role in Dad's death.

The shame of robbing the world of an honorable man.

The blame of creating a widow and leaving her to suffer her loss by herself.

He lifted his head and looked in front of him to the edge of the dock. The water's surface rippled violently with each rain drop.

He visualized him and Dad standing there so many years ago.

His arms extended in front of him, gripping the wet wooden planks with his fingers.

Pulling toward redemption.

Aiden stood up and stumbled to the edge of the dock, standing for several moments as he looked down.

The water raged against the dock, battering the surface but washing away the filth.

His mind was flooded with images of Dad's car. The white roses on his casket. The cabin sitting empty for so many years.

The water was an end with the promise of a beginning.

So much of Aiden's story was monstrous. What he needed was something divine.

He dove head-first into the water.

It was cold. Excruciatingly cold, even after standing on the dock for so long. He curled his legs up to his chest and wrapping his arms around them. It was as if a thousand needles were shoved into his skin and had made their way into his soul.

He accepted the pain.

He remained underwater for several moments, slowly letting his arms and legs hang suspended. Underwater, his inner demons and self-deprecating voices faded away and were drowned out by the blood pounding through his ears. Freeing himself of guilt, of secrecy, of lies.

He kicked his legs and rose to the surface, taking a huge gasp for air.

Fresh air.

Aiden's lungs had never felt so effective, so clear. He swam over to the dock and held his back against the wooden edge, facing the water with his arms stretched out to either side. He rested his head on the wood, closed his eye and let his lower body hang loose in the water as his head and arms were bathed by the rain.

Aiden's world stood still. He had rid himself of his pain. Traces of pain would remain.

He accepted this.

There was no guilt this morning at Lake Providence. Here, there was peace.

For once, there was peace.

Aiden rested in the here and now. He was present.

Naked.

Unashamed.

Wild.

Free.

PART II

19. FIRST FRUITS

Nature undergoes significant transformation between November and April. Trees are stripped of their leaves and appear more grey than brown. The whole world seems grey.

Such is life during a Pacific Northwest winter. What's often referred to as one of the most livable regions on the continent for three quarters of the year passes through a dark period of overcast sky, damp winds and – more notoriously – torrential rain. The latter keeps you cooped up inside so as to remain dry and untouched by this unfortunate act of nature. When it does let up for a day or so, traces remain in the surrounding nature: muddy roads, standing water and washed-up debris.

It's a mess of a world.

Come late March, a new world begins to form. Trees that stand saturated from months of rain are exposed to slight but consistent increases of temperature, causing them to mould. Yet this mould isn't an end; it's the start of a new life. Where the overwhelming grey world is dispelled by hints of green moss. Moss is to spring what rain is to winter: the be all, end all.

The shadow of winter makes one long for the promise of beauty that's evident in the remaining seasons through the rebirth of the natural world.

Nature's prima donna.

Spring weather was slowly overtaking Cielo. Leaves were beginning to grow and buds were starting to open. Newness was in the air.

Aiden felt the newness today as he pedaled Dad's old bike down Canoe Drive toward the Borough. He had discovered the bike behind the cabin in December, leaning against the exterior wall collecting dust and rust. Dwayne, the local mechanic, helped him refurbish the seat and handlebars and oil the gears and chain back to usability. Now that spring had rolled around, the car had little appeal to Aiden. Biking let him save on gas and see the world.

His time on Cielo had brought him to care enough to actually see the world. To want it. To experience nature's metamorphosis.

Aiden had let his hair grow out, now hanging about three inches above his shoulders. Still couldn't succeed at a full beard but he did what he could. His dirty blond curls blew in the wind as he rode his bike. The scruff made Aiden appear more mature but far younger at heart.

For someone who had lived his life behind walls of insecurity, letting his hair grow long blew in the face of safety and protection. The decision was subtle, unconscious. This was his own spring after a life-long winter.

Never had Aiden felt such liberation than after that fateful evening at Lake Providence. It was his first step toward authentic community, even if that community only consisted of him and another: Rosemary. Their stories, while entirely different, were a shared narrative of restored humanity. The aftermath of human brokenness walking together.

While they did indeed learn from each other, it was Aiden who gleaned the most from the shared friendship.

Perhaps "mentorship" is a better word.

That was Rosemary's role in Aiden's life as he learned to properly grieve the loss of his father and accept his role in Dad's passing. He had bypassed bargaining and denial through his outward anger, and depression had been a subtle undertone ever since the funeral, keeping him in a self-contained prison.

But Rosemary wouldn't allow Aiden to wallow in depression. She pushed him out of self-pity toward acceptance.

Aiden laid low during Christmas, passing the holiday by himself despite an invitation from Rosemary. She pressed him to join her for dinner at her house for Easter. This time, he gladly accepted.

After much convincing from Rosemary, Aiden took to gardening. Never one to take up a hobby; he didn't have the drive, passion, interest or commitment. He much preferred buying what was already available.

Truthfully, Aiden hated his hands getting dirty.

He owed it to Rosemary to give it a chance.

The initial pursuit brought with it frustration and repeated failures, wilted leaves and invasive weeds. He didn't have the patience to keep up the necessary maintenance.

With Rosemary's mentorship in progress, though, he stuck with it. He pulled out the weeds and the leaves stayed intact. For a few months, the plants seemed to be hanging on.

Aiden was meeting with Rosemary on her 20-minute afternoon break today. With a slight turn of the handlebars, he steered the bike left onto Borough Boulevard. Hopped off the bike and walked it over the bike stand at The Bean House, which had become his choice caffeine supplier on Cielo.

He was looking forward to today's get-together.

He arrived about 10 minutes before their meeting was due, so he ordered his long-pour Americano and snatched up the in-house copy of *The Seattle Times*. Stories of political campaigns, localized crimes and international affairs. All significantly relevant to the respective stories' geographical settings but entirely irrelevant this morning on Cielo.

That's what Aiden had come to appreciate most about island living – the lack of connection to the world's problems.

Or his past.

Even better.

He sipped his coffee, the drink warming his throat on the way down.

The door's bell rang just as Aiden finished perusing the cover page. In walked Rosemary.

She walked toward the counter where she ordered a cup of chamomile tea, requesting a teaspoon of honey to be stirred in.

They sat at their usual table by the window with a panoramic view of The Borough.

"I've got some news," he said.

"Yes?"

"I went outside this morning while the coffee was brewing. Stretched, took in the morning air, glanced over at the garden."

She nodded.

Aiden leaned forward, eyes slightly widened.

"Two tomatoes," he said.

Rosemary merely smiled, a subtle congratulations.

"I did it Rosemary, I did it!" he said, slamming his palms on the table top.

"Well that's a great start! You put a lot of work into that plant, and it certainly paid off."

She stirred the tea and brought the maroon mug to her mouth.

"Sure did," he proudly agreed.

"But I wouldn't get too cocky," she warned, both hands holding her tea as the steam rose.

His eyes quickly widened as his head pulled back.

"Why not?" he asked. "It grew, now it's just gotta get a little fatter."

"Oh, the ignorance of youth," she said, grinning as she looked out of the window.

"Now who's being cocky?" he said with a straight face. While Rosemary often had the upper hand when it came to wisdom, Aiden had learned to stand his ground.

"Aiden, that plant could die far more quickly than you'd think. One bad weed or a bug infestation will eat through the stems and the fruit will fall right off with no hope of recovery. Be proud of what you've accomplished, but don't think the pursuit stops there."

She took another drink of her tea.

"Point taken," he responded.

"But you have learned the ways of the land. You

should be seeing some of the other plants take a few steps forward soon enough."

"That's what I'm hoping for. Maybe even selling some in town when the time comes."

Rosemary looked on proudly. Her lessons in the garden often resulted in Aiden's frustration, but she wouldn't let him give up. And he didn't. He pressed on with it.

"You've got an awful lot to be proud of, Aiden. You took on a challenge and you stuck with your commitment in the face of a lot of frustration and defeats. You're seeing the fruit of your labors now."

Aiden smiled with humble sincerity.

"This is the first time I've had anything to be proud of," he said. "Dad would've been proud to see me sticking to something."

"I wasn't just talking about the tomato plant," she said.

"Neither was I."

Their agreement floated in the air for several moments.

Aiden's memory shifted back to Dad's letter.

"I pray, son, that you will reclaim your right to greatness."

"Guess he got his dying wish then," Aiden said, breaking the silence.

She looked at her watch. "Well, break's about over," she said, rising from the table. "Till we meet again, Mr. Lawrence."

"Till then, Ms. Friesen."

Aiden downed the rest of his coffee, took their cups up to the counter and stepped outside onto the wooden porch, noticing the moss growing between the planks.

He sighed a sigh of contentment, acknowledging the new growth sprouting up across the island.

Victory over winter.

Aiden smiled each time he saw the moss.

20. PICK YOUR TEAM

Another week had gone by, clocking in at more than six months on Cielo. But these last months had flown by. Aiden's projects kept him busy.

Main focus? The cabin property.

He could do some minor tasks himself. Raking up debris, adding plants to the yard, planting grass and laying gravel.

Most tasks required Chase. He had long since finished the initial renovations. Roof, deck, counter tops and appliances. Yet there was always something to improve, in Aiden's opinion.

He also realized that any potential buyer would need more space than was currently available.

The solution? A storage shed. Nothing massive, just functional.

That's how Aiden described it when he contracted the job out to Chase.

Aiden returned from a morning bike ride shortly after Chase got to cabin. It started raining not long after he began his ride, cutting the excursion a bit short.

Chase had already cleared the 8x10 plot behind the cabin and set the foundation last week. He was here to build the frame today.

As he rode his bike into the driveway, Aiden saw that Chase had stacked the 2x4s in separate piles, set up a table saw on a plank supported by two sawhorses and had already begun cutting the six-foot frame pieces.

Aiden dismounted his bike and watched from a distance as Chase ran the wooden planks through the saw, sawdust caught in the breeze and settling on his perspiring arms.

Small talk never seemed to be the winning ticket with Chase, so Aiden thought it best to engage him professionally rather than personally.

"Is it safe to use the saw in the rain?" Aiden asked.

"Just sprinkles," Chase responded without breaking his stare. "Trees block the water enough."

The conversation had already turned to weather patterns. Never a good sign.

"Foundation's all set?" he asked as soon as the saw was disengaged.

"Think I'd be here otherwise?" he replied, disinterested in Aiden's presence.

Flawless craftsmanship, horrid people skills. Aiden had come to expect this of Chase.

Still hard to believe this cold-blooded loner was related to Rosemary.

Aiden wasn't exactly sure why he felt a need to talk to Chase. Maybe he just wanted approval.

He always wanted approval.

"Sounds good to me, so long as it's finished before winter," he said.

Chase stepped away from the saw and faced Aiden, flexing his broad shoulders.

"Like you're in any kind of a rush anymore," he scoffed.

"Beg your pardon?"

Chase wiped his forehead with the back of his hand, sawdust mixing with his sweat.

"Another day, another thing to build," Chase said, laying the wood on the ground and joining them together at their respective corners with a nail gun.

A series of gunshot-like sounds erupted through the still afternoon air as the nails shot into the two boards.

Apparently the ice was thick as ever, Aiden thought.

"And this is inconveniencing you how?" Aiden asked when the shots subsided, decidedly through with trying to make conversation.

"No issue. You just can't make up your mind. Don't know what you want."

Within a minute, the first frame was assembled. Chase lifted the finished frame and dropped it into the holder sticking out of the foundation.

"I'm making up my mind plenty," Aiden said. "Lots needs to get done around here for the property to be ready to sell."

"Please," Chase said, repeating the same process with another set of planks. "You're just as indecisive as the first day you showed up on the island. No clue where you're headed."

"I'd say these renovations show pretty clearly where I'm headed," Aiden said, making a fist with his thumb out and motioning behind him. "Out of here."

"When I started working on this place you couldn't wait to get away," Chase said.

He dropped the second frame perpendicular to the

one he had already placed. "Now you can't get through a month without thinking up another project."

"This is my project, not yours," Aiden said, looking Chase straight in the eye. "Maybe I'll leave this summer, maybe I'll stay till the place sells. My property, my decision."

"My apologies, lord of the land."

"Don't give me that crap," Aiden retorted.

Chase held his gaze, but his lips curled into to sadistic smile.

"If you're so peeved about what I have to say – which you know I'll say regardless – why do you keep hiring me?"

"You get the job done and you do it well, apart from being a douche bag."

Chase let the silence hang in the air for several seconds.

"You're getting roped in," he said.

Aiden had no clue what he was referring to.

"Roped in?"

"You like it here," Chase said, "and you're gonna stay. That's why you're putting so much work into this place."

Aiden felt a knot tighten in his stomach. He didn't know why.

Chase assembled the two remaining frames quickly and gave them their place along with the others.

"You're putting it off," he added.

Aiden was confused.

"Who said anything about staying?"

"No one had to."

Chase walked over to the lumber pile and picked up a large sheet of particle board, already cut to fit the side of the shed. Scaled it up against the frame and secured it with the nail gun.

Six consecutive shots rang through the air, each one piercing the air with strong force.

Chase grabbed a second board and matched it with the other frame.

"You're gonna get all warm and cozy with a select few, make some friends, then bolt when the going gets tough."

Another six shots.

"Say," he said, "isn't that how you got here?"

Aiden knew enough about Chase to know he only cared about getting under people's skin. He had fallen victim to it before. Not this time.

"Cielo is where I'm at right now," Aiden said. "I cut things off for a reason and I'm better for it. I'm moving forward, and I'm not going to waste my life with cynicism anymore."

He walked past Chase toward the cabin's porch, then turned around to look Chase in the eye.

"You should try it sometime," he said as he opened the front door to walk in.

"At least bring some integrity to your optimism and be straight about it," Chase shouted across the driveway, unloading the sheet metal with which to construct the roof.

"Pick your team," Chase yelled. "You can't crap in two cans at the same time."

21. STRAY

It was an unusually warm spring day. No clouds in the sky to block the sun from bathing the island with its rays. A cold night would likely follow, but for the moment, it was warm.

Aiden's sub-conscience had become defined by existing in the moment, in one particular space of time.

This particular moment found him on his bike. He had started to take upon himself the adventure of discovering new parts of the island whenever the weather permitted.

Venturing off the beaten path sometimes led to a clearing in the woods, sometimes to a vast meadow, sometimes to an ocean view. Other times, it left him in the woods just to walk.

Aiden loved walking more than anything as it combined exercise, leisure, meditation and isolation. A time for personal reflection while moving silently through the busy world, completely at home with oneself in the midst of countless strangers or natural surroundings. Simply being alive.

He recalled reading a Henry David Thoreau book that described walkers as not having any particular home but feeling at home everywhere.

Aiden pulled his bike over and leaned it against a tree, preparing himself to be at home wherever today's walk might lead. He walked through the dense covering, sticks cracking under his feet and occasional branches catching his hair.

Moments later, Aiden stumbled across a small pond with an island – about six feet wide – in the middle. On that island stood a weeping willow tree, its long branches extending down over the water's surface.

An oasis. A peaceful home.

Quiet.

Something he had been longing for since his last encounter with Chase. His accusations were starting to rub Aiden the wrong way. Chase didn't seem to know where the line was.

But Chase wasn't here today. Just Aiden.

Something else was in the area, too. He heard something swishing in the water behind the willow tree. An animal, perhaps.

What he saw instead was a familiar face. Onyx, the spice-selling hippie from the market, swimming with just his head above the water's surface.

Not too far from an animal, Aiden reasoned.

"Thought you were a stray dog," he said. "Mind a visitor?"

Onyx quickly stood up, water just above his waist, revealing his bare upper half.

Must not have heard Aiden walk up.

"Good guess," he said, smiling. "And no, don't mind at all."

Aiden sat down on a flat rock. It hadn't rained in a couple days, but the soil was still damp.

"What's this place?" he asked. "Public property?"

"Private lot," Onyx said. "Really nice house just through there." He pointed to the left.

"They here now?"

"Nope. Rich couple's summer home. When the cat's away," he said, spreading his arms wide, "the mouse will play!"

With that, he leaned back into the water, completely submerged.

Aiden waited for him to resurface. "So trespassing isn't too frowned upon here?"

Onyx ran both hands through his long brown hair, combing it back with his fingers. Shook his head in response.

"What are you doing here, then?" Aiden asked.

"This pond was here way before any property lines were set," Onyx said, moving toward the shallow end of the pond. "No harm in taking a little swim."

He walked out of the water, completely naked and unaware of social norms.

Aiden wasn't surprised in the least; he turned and saw Onyx's pile of clothes close by.

"Need a towel?" Aiden asked, looking at the ground. He'd grown comfortable with his own skin, but Onyx was too comfortable for Aiden's liking.

Onyx looked taken aback, then glanced down.

"Oh, my bad," he said, leaning over to grab his t-shirt. He covered his waist, sat down beside Aiden on another rock and then draped the shirt over himself, still too wet to dress.

The two men sat in the silence of the surrounding nature, each of them soaking in what serenity the area had to offer them. The air was still as a few bugs skimmed across the water's surface. The sun cut through the trees and reflected off the pond. Up above, chickadees chirped and flew from tree to tree, searching for lunch.

"Long time no see, by the way," Onyx said.

"Amen to that," Aiden replied. While Rosemary had become a dear friend, Aiden felt a certain fondness toward Onyx. Onyx was quirky and oftentimes far-fetched, but Aiden found that an appealing quality in a friend.

"How've you been keeping?" Aiden finally asked.

"Fairly busy. Sales slow down in the off season but I'm getting ready for the tourist surge in a couple months. Man, once they're here, the whole island is swamped. Great for business, but tiring man, tiring."

"I can imagine," Aiden said.

"Been thinking of taking my stuff over to a few shops on Sandman Island. Wouldn't require much more man power, and it could generate some more business in the winter months. Maybe get some good momentum started this fall."

"Well if you need help developing a business model down the road, consider me an asset," Aiden said.

"And what would you know about that?"

"Studied it in school," Aiden said. "Got another year or so to finish the degree. Still got the head knowledge, though."

"Well who knows," Onyx said, using his elbows to support himself as he leaned back. "Maybe you could help me out."

Aiden laughed. "It's an offer. How about if we hash out some ideas next week?"

"Will do. Meet me at Fisherman's Bluff next Friday around 5. North end of Cielo."

"Done."

"So you're still gonna be kicking around? Thought you said something about selling and then leaving the island."

"That was the plan," Aiden said. "Still lots of stuff to do around the property, getting it ready. Started a garden, actually."

"You did?"

"Sure thing," he said. "A few tomatoes are coming up now."

"Well I'll be damned!" Onyx said, raising his right hand for a high-five. Aiden awkwardly reciprocated.

"Rosemary Friessen helped me with it," Aiden said. "Didn't think I'd make it – never would've thought I'd wanna grow anything. But I tell you, it was awesome to see something actually come out of it. Rewarding, to say the least."

"She's an exceptional lady," Onyx said. "Helped me get my stuff on the shelves at the store. Owe her a lot. She invites a group of us lonely misfits each year for Easter dinner. Potluck style."

"Well I'll see you there this year," Aiden said.

He looked out again at the willow tree. More and more he was finding himself captivated by nature's raw beauty. He could happily sit here for hours gazing at the willow, discovering an entirely new scene each passing hour as the sun's changing angle cast a different hue on the tree.

"Who's gonna take care of 'em when you leave?" Onyx asked.

"What?" he asked.

"These plants," he said. "You put so much work into them, so you're obviously not just gonna let 'em wilt and die. You adding that into your screening process for buyers?"

"Guess I never thought about that," Aiden said, scratching his left knee.

"Then I suggest you do," Onyx said, taking the shirt off his waist and standing up by Aiden's side. He pulled up grey khaki shorts and fastened his belt.

"Guess I'll cross that bridge when I come to it. There's always more to improve on. I'll probably stick it out till everything's in place."

Onyx used his shirt to dab off his chest and arms, then pulled the shirt sleeves through a belt loop.

"You sure seem to be putting your roots down here," he said. "Not just in that little garden of yours."

Aiden got off the ground and brushed the debris off his backside. He picked up a small rock and tossed it into the pond.

It made a subtle splash.

He ran his hand through his hair, pulling it out of his eyes.

"Not gonna lie, I'm starting to see myself here more and more."

Onyx casually walked over to the pond's edge.

"Long term?" he asked.

"I don't want to think about anything permanent right now," Aiden answered. "I'm just enjoying this new season. Passing through."

Onyx let out a laugh. "Now who's the stray dog?"

Aiden laughed in return. "Don't I at least pass as a welcomed guest at this point? Unless I wear out my welcome, of course."

Slipping into his sandals before walking into the densely wooded forest, Onyx turned to face Aiden with a grin. "'Tis the eventual fate of all strays, ain't it?"

22. THREE VOICES

For every sunny day in the northwest, three rainy days are likely to follow. Aiden was happy that today was on the closing end of the rain. The land was still saturated from the night before; steam rose steadily from every surface as the morning sun made its assent into the sky.

Chase was scheduled to come over in the afternoon to finish off the storage shed and attach the metal roof. An hour at most, he told Aiden, adding that he wanted Aiden there in person to sign off on the shed's completion.

In the meantime, Aiden was looking forward to harvesting the fruit of his labor. His garden had sprung up with artichokes, garlic and lemons. He knew several recipes that called for marinated artichoke hearts, and his crop had reached maturity.

Aiden had just finished getting dressed when he heard Rosemary riding in on her bike, resting the bike against the waterproof-stained deck. Beads of water covered the deck's surface from last night's rain, each bead quivering as it made contact with the wooden railing.

He checked his watch. 10 o'clock. Right on time.

Two knocks on the door before Rosemary turned the brass handle from the opposite side.

"A fine day for a harvest," she said to Aiden as she opened the door.

"We can harvest later," he said, stepping aside so she could come in. "Tea comes first."

Rosemary smiled. "You've learned well, Mr. Lawrence."

She removed her shoes and left them near the front steps before hanging her overcoat behind the door. She then pulled a chair up to the small oak table. Two tea cups sat next to each other on the table's top.

Aiden filled a metal tea kettle with tap water and placed it on the stove element, turning the dial to high heat. He then opened up a cupboard door, pulling out a small tin.

"Earl Grey?" he asked.

"Fine, thanks," she responded.

Aiden dropped two tea bags into a porcelain pot. Steam whistled through the kettle's spout within minutes. He added the hot water, stirred with a spoon and brought it to the table, letting it steep.

"You've turned into quite a host," Rosemary noted.

"Seven bucks for the two pots and the cups. Thrift store had it all."

"Never did fancy you as a thrifty shopper."

"Seasons of change, remember?" Aiden said with a smile.

"Yes, yes. Very good."

He lifted the porcelain pot and poured tea into Rosemary's cup. He did the same for his own.

Often times their conversations would pick up right quickly, cutting through surface-level chit chat.

Today, they both welcomed the silence in the cabin's warm ambiance.

Rosemary looked around the space, noticing the renovations.

"The kitchen is beautiful," she said.

They sipped their tea in silence.

"I feel good," Aiden said, breaking the silence after five minutes. "Best I've ever felt."

He paused.

"Regardless of what comes next, I know what has passed. For that, I'm happy."

"Passed?" Rosemary asked as she brought her cup to her mouth.

"Everything," he said. "The guilt, the shame, the secrets. I came to Cielo to close off loose ends, and it ended up opening all these wounds for the first time. I thought I was going to lose it. Literally."

Aiden took a deep sip of his tea.

"My tight grip was slipping, losing its grasp on everything I had tried to control. And I was sick of it, Rosemary. I was so, so sick of it."

"And you're happy now?"

"I said it, didn't I?"

"Are you happy with letting things be and not trying to control them anymore?"

"I said I'm happy," Aiden answered quickly. "That covers it."

She said nothing. She neither objected nor affirmed.

For such an eloquent woman, Rosemary's occasional silences took Aiden by surprise.

He had learned to let the moment pass.

Aiden realized he was holding his tea cup too tight.

Almost burnt his hands. He set his cup down on its saucer.

"It's time for lady wisdom to do some learning herself," Aiden said, quickly changing the topic.

"Beg your pardon?"

"Outside," he said, rising from the table with purpose.

They slipped on their shoes and walked out to the garden patch.

"Aiden," Rosemary said, as they stood over the plants. "What are we doing out here?"

"You're getting your first cooking lesson today."

"Seriously?" she asked, subtle shock visibly spreading across her face. "I thought we were in the middle of a conversation back there."

"For all the knowledge you have, and for everything you've said to me, I know you've still got some space in that brain of yours. Today, you learn how to cook. I know you make your big meals at Thanksgiving and Easter and Christmas, but we're going gourmet now."

"But I've never —"

"Oh, that changes today! No way you're getting out of it," he said with a grin. She stared down at the patch, still unable to assemble a proper sentence.

Aiden had finally left Rosemary speechless.

"Were gonna marinate some artichoke hearts and I've got all the ingredients here. Nothing too extreme to start out with, but tasty nonetheless. Let's get going with it."

He pulled two full artichokes out of the soil along with a head of garlic and a few parsley stems. Together they walked back inside to the kitchen. Aiden rinsed off the artichoke heads in the sink, cutting one in half from the top down.

"Here's your basic anatomy of an artichoke," he said. "Outer leaves, stem and heart. Cut off the stem and peel back those leaves, about four layers in."

Carefully taking the knife and the other artichoke, she sliced through the thick stem and pulled off the leaves.

"And now the other," he said, passing the second vegetable to her.

To her surprise, she successfully repeated the process.

"Perfect, now put the hearts in here," Aiden said, indicating a nearby bowl on the counter top.

"Now for the key component of any gourmet dish: fresh garlic. Pull two or three cloves out, then press down with the flat side of your knife." He took the knife to demonstrate and cracked off the outer peel.

"Your turn," he said.

Rosemary quickly cracked the other two cloves much to her own surprise.

Next, she diced up the garlic and parsley.

"Hey, I haven't messed up yet!" she said with a confident smile. "My kitchen endeavors usually consist of grabbing cutlery for microwave dinners."

"First stop, Aiden's kitchen. Next stop, Food Network," Aiden said, patting her on the back. "But we're not done yet."

He opened the small standing pantry and pulled out two glass bottles.

"Half cup of wine vinegar, half cup of olive oil," he said, pointing to the bottles.

"Pour those into the bowl, along with the hearts, garlic and parsley."

She combined all the ingredients, after which he secured the container with an airtight lid.

"Pick it up and shake it all around," Aiden politely ordered; Rosemary obeyed.

"And that's it!" he said.

"Time to eat now?"

"Not today, sadly. They're much better the next day. Far more flavor."

A soft sound rumbled outside. Aiden turned to look through the kitchen window. He loved the visual escape when performing a monotonous chore like washing the dishes.

He saw that Chase's truck was parked in the gravel lot.

Aiden looked at his watch. Already 11:30.

He watched as Chase got out of the truck and pulled the sheet metal from the truck bed, his arms visibly contacting through a fitted grey t-shirt.

"You going to greet him?" Rosemary asked, herself peering through the window.

Aiden shook his head.

"We don't talk much," he said. "I've tried. We're not exactly two peas in a pod."

"Oh, my nephew wouldn't fit in a pod with anyone," she said, shaking her head. "So talented, but dreadfully impersonal."

"Understatement of the year," he said. "He gets the job done but any time I've tried to engage him in conversation, it ends up as some sort of attack."

Aiden watched Chase as Rosemary turned to face Aiden.

"Attack?" she asked.

He squinted as he formed the words.

Rosemary waited.

"Claiming that I don't know what I'm talking about, or that I can't make my mind up about anything."

"With all your talk just now, I assumed you no longer perceived criticism as an attack," she said. "Seems to be rather trivial feedback."

"Maybe at the surface, but he prods," he said, pausing. "He prods where he has no business doing so."

"Isn't that what I do best?" she asked with a subtle laugh.

Aiden bit his lower lip, searching for the right words to explain his feelings.

"It's...it's different with Chase. I can see the good in most people. You, for example, annoyed the daylight out of me when we first met. But your words resonated with me. Gave some positive direction. With Chase, I don't see anything redemptive in him. Hard to even see a soul."

Again, Rosemary held her silence. Aiden was beginning to wonder what she was trying to articulate with these silences.

He turned back to the table, pouring another cup of tea for Rosemary.

"If anything, I've learned that it's all about picking my battles," he said. "Not much good will come from battling with him and I'm fine with that."

Two loud knocks rang from the door through the cabin. Aiden turned and opened the door. Chase stood on the other side of the frame, sweating through his shirt.

"Roof's done," he said before turning and walking toward the shed with a hammer in his hand.

Aiden followed.

The shed looked great. Storage space to house whatever an owner may wish to keep outside the cabin but protected from the elements.

From the buyer's perspective, he knew there had to be something else that might improve the shed. Something that would add a bit more versatility. To make it less of a shed and more of a secondary cabin.

Maybe he wasn't even thinking about the buyer's perspective.

Perhaps his second-guessing was more so an attempt to push back. To take the pilot's seat and determine the scenario's course. To execute a vendetta, even. To look down on the macho carpenter and bring about submission.

"Windows," he finally said.

"Windows?"

"Yes," Aiden said. "Windows. Two on each side. Double pane."

This spur of confidence came out of nowhere, and he was running with it. Aiden could finally use Chase's demeaning rants as motivation for reciprocity.

Aiden had never been able to lord over his superiors, but that changed today.

Superiors?

Was Chase even a superior?

Or was it all in his head?

"You want me to cut through the finished sidings and install two insulated windows, when the structure is already done?"

"What, is that beyond your abilities?" Aiden asked.

"Bloody hell," Chase responded, throwing the hammer into the dirt.

"Nothing personal, just think it could use some natural lighting," Aiden said. "Whoever buys the property may be looking for higher quality than a mere shack."

"This 'mere shack' is what you requested, and I'll be damned if you keep wasting my time on your menial indecisiveness and lack of backbone," Chase scathed.

Aiden had struck a nerve with Chase. This fed Aiden's strength.

"Who's the one writing your paychecks?" he demanded. "Who's been keeping you employed these past months when work slowed down? I have."

Chase took three steps closer to Aiden, his shoulder muscles contracting and eyes narrowing.

"Listen up," he said. "Don't even think of trying to paint yourself as some supporter of the working man. You haven't worked in years thanks to Daddy's inheritance and you'd be dead broke without that. I work for my livelihood, and that gives me every right to pick and choose my own work. You got money? Good for you, but I don't need this."

Aiden constricted. Fists and stomach tightened. Blood pulsed through his temples.

His tongue failed to form words.

He felt weak.

His strength fled as quickly as it appeared.

He panicked.

"You don't talk to —"

"Grow up you two," a third voice said from the cabin's steps.

Rosemary stood on the cabin steps with one hand on the rail, looking disgusted. "I may be old but I'm not so old that I can't hear childish bickering."

"Stay out of this, Rosemary," Aiden said, his voice shaking. He couldn't make eye contact with her. He knew he was in over his head.

"I've got this under control," he said quietly.

"Do you, Aiden?" she asked, disgust turning to concern. "Do you?"

Sweat beaded along his brow. Chase stood there without acknowledging Rosemary.

"I've got this under control," he repeated, looking at the ground.

"What the hell makes you think you've got the right to control anything?" Chase said, staring directly at Aiden. "You spend what, six months on the island and you think you can control it? Control me? You're pathetic."

He spit at Aiden's feet.

"That's enough, Chase," Rosemary interjected, stepping off the deck and walking between the two men.

She looked at Chase. "There's no need for this," she said. "You've done your work, now either carry on or leave."

Chase smiled sadistically, rubbed his hands together and spread his arms out. "You've got it," he said, then turning to look at Aiden. "Cut your own damn windows."

With that, he got into his truck and drove off. Aiden couldn't move from his stance in the driveway. He stared at the dirt. He couldn't figure out how he lost all courage so quickly.

Rosemary walked over to him, placing her left hand on his right shoulder. He felt rigid.

Cold.

Empty.

"Care to tell me what that was all about?" she asked.

He continued to stare at the ground.

"I hate that soulless jerk," he finally said.

Her hand held its place. She searched for the words to say.

"Come see me at the store tomorrow," she said, walking over to her bike. "Noon. Don't be late."

23. LOOSENED STITCH

From peaceful serenity to emotional relapse in one fleeting moment.

How had it happened?

Aiden pondered this all evening. Not since his first night on Cielo had he felt so alone with these questions; not since right before that fateful dip in Lake Providence had he so strongly felt the presence of his own demons and vices.

How had he returned to this destructive mindset after experiencing such freedom and peace?

He thought he may know why.

No, he knew.

Was he ready to face the reason?

Hardly.

"Come see me at the store tomorrow," Rosemary had said. *"Don't be late."*

Aiden checked the clock. 11:42. Time to go.

He was still in yesterday's jeans, sandals and crew-cut shirt. He had fallen asleep at the kitchen table and woke up this morning with a crook in his neck. Slowly rolled his head from one shoulder to the other before exiting the cabin and getting in the car.

Ten minutes later, he was in the store parking lot in front of its large A-frame window.

Through the window he saw Rosemary carefully placing a customer's groceries into their own re-usable shopping bag.

She looked up from the till and caught his eyes as he sat in the car, kindly acknowledging his presence.

Aiden got out of the car without locking the door.

He waited outside the store's entrance, observing the clippings on a large bulletin board. Dog-sitting ads, realtor listings, community events. Could be a decent place to eventually advertise the cabin.

Rosemary walked through the doors, one hand in the pocket of her vest and the other holding a travel mug.

"Glad to see you made it," she said.

Aiden held off on eye contact, merely nodding his head in acknowledgment.

"Where we headed?" he asked.

"Let's walk," she said, moving past him toward the road. He followed.

They made their way over to a small park across the street. Rosemary sat on a lone wood bench, which stood next to two rhododendron bushes and a cherry blossom tree.

Most of the blossoms had blown onto the surrounding grass, mixed with the soil. The tree was mostly bare.

Aiden joined her on the bench, resting his elbows on his knees.

Rosemary twisted the lid off of her travel mug, tilting it into his line of vision.

"Is this partially full, or mostly empty?" she asked.

Aiden looked, seeing the small amount of coffee left in the mug. "Few swigs left," he said.

"To say it's partially full, you have to provide argument as to why the situation is more positive than negative," she said. "Optimism requires convincing. But pessimism, however small, gets the spotlight."

"This really isn't the time for your –"

"Look over there," she interrupted, pointing toward a white-washed church adjacent to the store. "The purest white, almost blinding to the eye. That's how it looks from over here. But if you walk closer, you see a baseball-size black scuff on the lower right hand corner of the wall. 'Wow, what a shame,' you'd say. The only thing you'd notice is the scuff. And this tiny blemish has the power to take away from all of the white."

"That's enough, Rosemary!"

She continued without regarding his comments. "Cynicism quickly dismisses the white of the wall and makes the small scuff more important. This scuff is problematic because it has damaged the integrity of the wall. A once pure structure, flawed just like you and me. It's a realistic perspective, don't get me wrong. But it's easy to take on, and once you do, the world looks like one giant scuff."

"Focus on the good, got it," Aiden said spitefully.

"Optimism takes work, Aiden. Yes, there's ignorant optimism that negates the realities of the world and pretends that there are no problems – this is foolish and dangerous. Healthy optimism recognizes the flaws of our reality. Rather than ignoring them, it sees them as only a small part of the bigger picture. That black scuff is small. It's real, but it doesn't overwhelm the white. Genuine optimism understands that while problems are real, they scream at us and let us know that the world isn't running as it should – and optimism works to bring about full functionality once again. It's energized by hope and it strives for reconciliation."

Aiden stood up, ran his right hand through his hair and exhaled.

"Is that why you brought me here? To preach at me? What is it that you want?" Aiden demanded, his voice more desperate than irritated.

"It's not what I want that concerns me, Aiden. It's what I saw."

"And what did you see?"

"I saw the Aiden from several months ago," she said, speaking every single word with maternal conviction. "The Aiden who didn't trust, didn't love, didn't live. Those wounds may have healed some, but they're far from closed up. And the stitches are coming undone."

She hit the nail on the head. Aiden couldn't deny this.

He didn't try to.

Rosemary tucked a strand of hair behind her ear.

"You're not the only one with a past, Aiden."

"You don't have to tell me this again," he said. "We've talked about you already."

"I'm not talking about me. I'm talking about Chase."

He shrugged.

"What is there to tell? He's about as stoic as they come. And to be honest I could care less about his story."

"Stop it, Aiden. You're doing it again. Assuming that you're the only one with problems. You're not."

She took another sip from the travel mug.

"Chase was an only child of two young parents. They were the popular couple in high school, always in the prom court, the life of every party on the island. Everyone wanted to be them."

She adjusted her posture before continuing.

"She got pregnant their senior year. They both dropped out, tried to take the noble path of marriage. Determined to defy everyone's expectations of their pending failure."

A large truck drove past, its loud engine interrupting the conversation.

"They never grew up. The baby came a couple months after the modest wedding. Went through countless babysitters so they could spend most nights away. Drinking, snorting, everything. This continued for years. When they couldn't afford a babysitter anymore, they carried on at home – with Chase in the house."

She paused.

"On his sixth birthday, they told him they would celebrate the next night. Invited some kids over in advance. Had the place all decorated."

She adjusted the gold watch on her wrist.

"The following evening, around dinner time, kids started arriving. Knocked on the door repeatedly. No answer. But the truck was in the driveway. Concerned, one of the fathers present went around the back and kicked the door in. He asked if anyone was there. Again, no answer. He walked through the kitchen and saw a frosted cake on the kitchen counter, six unlit candles on top."

She paused again.

"When he turned to the living room, he saw a

brightly decorated room, streamers hanging from the ceiling and birthday plates on the table. Four empty bottles stood on the table. One plate had a small straw on it. Next to the straw was a razor blade, lined with white powder. To the left of the table were two bodies. Still. Cold."

Rosemary zipped up her vest and pulled her sleeves down.

"The father yelled for the parents to keep the other kids out side. A second father ran in and, seeing the two bodies, ran to the second door. Chase had to be in the house somewhere. They opened every door, searching for the boy. They finally got to the guest bathroom. Sitting behind the shower curtain was Chase. Looked like he'd been sitting there all night. His face was blank, absent of any emotion."

Aiden realized he hadn't moved in the past five minutes. His shoulders were tight. He stretched them back, easing the tension.

"Chase spent years bouncing around different foster homes," Rosemary continued. "He was placed with decent families. He excelled in school, was the brightest student in his class. He graduated and moved out on his own shortly after, getting a job with a local carpenter. He learned the trade and stuck with it ever since. But he never warmed up or spoke about that night. Ever."

She looked to the grass at her feet.

"Chase made a future for himself. He may seem heartless and cold, but he used that unfathomable pain to make himself stronger."

Rosemary then turned to Aiden.

"Chase is a lot stronger than you and me, Aiden, and only God knows what he's been through. We can do our best to put the past behind us. But just because it's behind us doesn't mean it no longer exists. We're all walking around carrying bits and pieces of our experiences. You can't ignore it. When you try to, it feels like it's buried away and gone. But our past will get tired of being pushed down. And when we least expect, it rears its ugly head and takes over."

She stopped.

"Aiden, it happened yesterday. We both know it."

He looked to the grass patch on his left. Two rabbits hopped around, seemingly at peace.

As a car drove by, they frantically jumped into a nearby bush.

"I thought I was past all this," he said. "That I finally dealt with it."

"You've coped, yes, but you haven't dealt. You're not Chase. You're not strong enough to repress your past like he did." She had never spoken with such rebuke. "You've got to make amends."

He was confused.

"Amends? With who?"

"Your father," she said.

"Rosemary, I'm not in the mood for sarcastic –"

"I'm dead serious," she interrupted. "This isn't a laughing matter. Your life is on the line, Aiden."

"How can you possibly be serious? He's dead. Been dead for more than a year."

"Think about it. What was it that turned your life around? What did you find?"

He paused to think.

"Dad's letter to me," he said.

"And have you reciprocated?"

"What the hell is that supposed to mean?" he said, his voice raised.

She stopped to catch her breath again. Adjusted her gold watch. Seemed to be a nervous habit.

"You may have felt resentment toward your father, but he never abandoned you or self-destructed in front of you on your birthday. He offered you love. He was tough on you, but he loved you."

Aiden ran his hand through his hair. "Where are you going with this?"

"Did that letter force you to look within yourself?" she asked.

He hated admission.

"Yes."

"Did it make you feel remorse?"

He hated vulnerability.

"Yes."

"Was that the moment that caused you to own up to your role in your father's death?"

He hated rebuke.

"Yes."

"And have you expressed that to him?"

He hated absurdity.

"How would I? He's dead!"

"Reconciliation is a two-way road. He reached out to you with that letter, Aiden. You've got to reach back to him."

"But he won't ever see it," he reasoned.

"This is for your own benefit, not mine," she said, standing up. "It at least could give you closure. Go to the cabin. Get yourself alone. Write. Write whatever you need to. Admit things left undone. Make it right."

Aiden spit to the side, wiping his mouth with the sleeve of his hoodie.

"This is ludicrous," he said. "What have I got to gain from writing to a dead man?"

She looked at her watch, standing up to leave. "You're not the cold type like Chase," she said, "but you're not stupid either. You can't sense decay if you've never tasted what it is to be alive – which you have, Aiden. Life is too short to live as a cynic, and you don't know when you'll be snatched away. You'll just stifle your soul every day you let this go by."

Rosemary walked back to the store. Aiden stayed on the bench.

He knew what he had to do.

24. DEAR DAD

The blank piece of paper screamed at Aiden. It appeared lifeless, laying still on Dad's wooden desk with a ballpoint pen to the side. An inanimate object with no physical ability to inflict harm.

Yet it knew that Aiden didn't have the will power to turn this blank sheet into a piece of reconciliatory communication with a living soul, let alone a dead man.

Aiden hadn't moved for the past hour. He'd lifted the pen multiple times but the page was still blank.

He lifted the pen.

"Hey," he started writing.

No, sounds too much like a text message. He scribbled it out.

"Dear Father."

No. Too formal. Had he ever said "Father"?

Aiden hardly remembered addressing Dad at all.

"Dear Dad."

No. Still too formal.

"Dear Gerald."

No. He hated it when kids addressed their parents by the first name.

With each failed attempt he scratched out the text. Didn't bother starting over on a new sheet of paper. He only had one sheet.

His thoughts shifted to Chase's story. Did Aiden honestly have any right to show disdain toward his father?

It was already a botched effort, and he knew it would be a botched end result. Still, he pressed on. He had to at least start without pretense, without formalities.

"Admit the things you left undone," Rosemary had said. *"Make it right."*

"Dad."

There. He had written that first word. It was only one, but it was one less that he still had to write.

"How are you?"

What was he thinking?! Dad was dead and six feet under, had been for more than a year.

"I don't know what I'm doing," he finally admitted. *"This letter, it doesn't make sense. You won't ever read this. No one will."*

"What's the point?" he wrote.

Aiden gripped the pen, then set it aside. He felt like a fool. Ran his hand through his hair, squinting his eyes.

He grabbed it again, slowly placing the point on the paper.

"It's my fault you'll never read this, Dad, and you don't even know why."

His breathing slowed, but the breaths were strong. Deep.

"I don't know how to say this," he continued, *"or even where to start."*

He had to keep writing, or he'd never finish.

"That night in Seattle. I had too much to drink."

He knew he couldn't start there. Had to start earlier. He scratched it out.

"I'm in the cabin right now. On Cielo Island. It's been a long time since I was here last. It was with you. You probably remember. Of course you do, it was one of the only trips we took together."

Tried to express some interest in the matter.

"We never went many places with Mom. It was hard on her to travel, with her health. That's why you took me to Cielo. To show me the cabin you built."

He struggled to take himself back to that moment on the dock. To that fishing lesson.

"I was 13. You said I was going to learn how to fish. We were on the dock at Lake Providence. I wasn't getting it. You tried to teach me but I couldn't get it. I...I was getting frustrated."

His eyebrows started to twitch.

"You had to cast the rod for me. Then I held it, and when I finally got a bite, I didn't reel it in fast enough. You tried again but it still didn't work."

He considered scratching out those last sentences. Maybe the detailed account wasn't that important.

But it was. He couldn't omit anything else. He had to keep going.

"I hate failing, Dad. I always have and you knew it."

He took another deep breath, his knuckles white from the tight grip.

"Why did you always force me to try things? Why did I have to be the best? I didn't want to learn how to fish 'cause I knew I wouldn't get it. And still, you pushed it."

He squinted, started rubbing his eyes. This wasn't right, this wasn't true.

"You pushed me. I gave up, and I blamed you for it."
Paused.

"I hated you for it."

Set down the pen, cracked his knuckles, picked it up again.

"That day. That day on the dock. I kept that memory and used it against you for years. Always blaming my shortcomings on your demands for greatness. It was my cop-out for not trying."

There were too many things to say, too many sentiments from over the years.

He had to get to the point.

"That night in Seattle, when I was in college. I called you, plastered drunk. I demanded you come pick me up, rescue me from the mess I got myself into. You wouldn't have it. You told me to solve my own problem and figure a ride out for myself. You stood up to me."

A tear streamed down his left cheek.

"I told you I hated you, that you were a lousy father. That if you loved me at all, you'd do what I wanted rather than me listen to your advice. You always had advice for me and I never wanted it. I always internalized it, hating you while trying to show some compliance. That night, I couldn't fake it. I flipped."

He scratched the back of his neck.

"So you came. You came to my rescue, and you died because of it. Because of me, because of my weakness, because of my failure. I..."

He paused, unable to complete the sentence.

Unable to articulate it.

He summoned the strength.

"...killed you."

He threw the pen across the room and crumpled the paper.

Tears followed.

Aiden sat in the desk chair for the next twenty minutes with limited movement, other than what flowed from his tear ducts.

Then he looked down at the crumpled paper. He grabbed it, carefully pressing it flat on the desk to straighten it out.

He reached for a second pen on the desk's surface.

"It was my fault," he wrote. *"It was all my fault."*

Tears continued to fall from his eyes onto the paper, smudging the ink.

"I'm sorry Dad." He paused. *"I'm so, so sorry. For everything. For twisting your love and care into some distorted victim complex. For pushing you away for so many years. For disrespecting you with every ounce of resentment I allowed to flood my thoughts. For demanding that you get me out of the mess I made, making you drive to your death."*

He stopped writing. The paper was wet.

"Mom doesn't know any of this. I couldn't let her know. She's had enough grief to deal with without knowing her son killed her husband."

He paused. Squinted his eyes.

"I love you Dad. I always have, I just never knew it. But you did. That's why you never stopped loving me. You knew I had it in me, that I'd someday find it."

Paused again.

"I want you to know something: I finally found it. And I owe it all to you, Dad. My path crossed with a local on Cielo and she called my bluffs just like you would have, but she directed me to community. To the light. To the truth. And it led me back to you. I just want you to know that, Dad,"

His eyes were dried with salt from the tears. They burned, but he didn't care.

"That's it."

He signed his name, put the pen down and got up. He needed to go for a bike ride, get some fresh air. He grabbed his hoodie, opened the door.

Stopped. Turned around and ran back to the desk. Grabbed the pen.

"P.S. I'm keeping the cabin."

25. INVENTORY

Aiden's bike ride led him into the Borough, occasional sun beams shooting down from the partly clouded sky. The ride took longer than usual. Aiden was drained – both emotionally and physically – from writing the letter, leaving minimal energy to keep the pedals moving.

The Bean House was his destination today.

He was exhausted yet relaxed. Something about that process gave closure. As if he had made peace with Dad.

But he didn't dwell on it.

Aiden positioned the bike against the building's backside, hidden enough so that a lock wasn't required. He had grown accustomed to leaving things unlocked.

Felt strange.

Almost liberating.

The wooden door triggered the bell atop the door jam. Several heads turned toward the entrance. Surprisingly crowded for a weekday morning, Aiden thought.

He walked up to the counter. Approached a young barista with a silk scarf wrapped in her brown hair.

"Large Americano, please," he said.

"Room for cream?"

"Sure."

The bean grinder made a loud but brief noise, dispensing grounds into the diffuser. She then fastened it to the espresso machine and placed two shot glasses under the spout, flipped a switch and let the machine do its work.

"Busy in here today," he commented.

"'Tis the season," she said, turning around to grab a paper cup. "Once the sun becomes an island resident, you can't keep them away." She looked past Aiden, nodding at the other customers.

He turned around subtly. Noticed their Spandex apparel and bike helmets. Cielo was one of the flatter islands in the region, making it a cyclist's oasis. Especially in the summer.

He turned back to the counter as the barista poured the espresso into the cup and filled it with hot water.

"$2," she said.

He pulled four crumpled dollar bills out of his pocket, then grabbed a copy of *The Cielo Platform* from a stack of newspapers on the counter.

"Keep the change."

Aiden added the cream, left and headed toward the water. The west side of the Borough had a few small strips of beach, each covered with rocks smoothed over by the gentle tide. Even with a growing summer population, Cielo's waterfronts still maintained an element of serenity. Much more likely to read in peace here than in a crowded coffee shop.

News was sparse in the paper, so he flipped to the classifieds. He spotted lots of ads promoting businesses, restaurants and professional services. Variety wasn't an issue; what was missing was a single attractive campaign.

Clearly neither vision nor creativity were invested into these ads. Maybe locals didn't care to rely on advertising campaigns or marketing strategy. News traveled by word of mouth, negating the need for much else. Cielo was a rather self-sustaining entity after all.

But there had to be some way of telling the story of Cielo in a better way, Aiden thought.

Even he could help these businesses refine their methods and draw a bigger crowd.

He pulled a pen from his pocket. Removed the cap and narrowed in on the first ad that caught his attention, trying to find something that stood out. Some sort of distinctive quality.

Spotted an ad for Harvest House, the restaurant that Rosemary frequented. Name written in a decent font, announcing its summer hours. A few new dishes. Availability for catering.

"Catering!" he thought. That was the golden ticket.

Wrote the word in the blank space to the left of the ad. Circled it. Drew two lines to the circle. Under the first, he wrote "summer season." The second, "special occasions."

"No," he said to himself. "Has to be something more specific."

Summer. Special occasions. What special occasions happen in the summer?

Picnics. Festivals. Weddings.

Weddings!

Localized, customized menu for a summer island wedding.

Did this kind of service even exist on Cielo? He looked at the other ads seeing nothing similar. The paper is only one ad space on the island, he realized, but certainly the most circulated.

He looked at his notes again. Pretty good, he thought. Maybe a new frontier for Harvest House.

If not new, at least refined. Better packaging on an existing product.

Looking back at his college classes, he knew enough to form a basic business plan.

Maybe he could pitch it to –

He stopped.

College classes? Thinking back to what he learned? Drawing on what he knew? Seeing if he had something to offer?

Advice?

Aiden had minimal experience in the way of consulting. A couple case studies, but only of student organizations on campus. Real-world clients were a different species altogether.

Why even entertain the thought of pursuing this?

Why not?

Aiden put the cap back on the pen.

Five minutes of scribbling had produced a marketable description. He imagined what he could do with some intentionality.

Dad had always pushed him to make something of himself.

Maybe he had it in him.

Onyx wanted to pick his brain for the spice business, so there must be something there.

Maybe that upcoming meeting would be a starting point.

A test.

Aiden downed his coffee, folded the paper and ran back to his bike. He had work to do.

Yes, work.

26. JOINT VENTURE

Friday finally arrived.

Aiden grew tired of twiddling his thumbs as he waited to meet up with Onyx. He never considered himself an expert, but with his mostly-completed business degree, he at least had something to offer.

A future in consulting as he drove.

A future. Rarely had that been part of his vocabulary.

Rarely had he any faith in himself.

Rarely had he perceived offering advice as a vocation.

That was about to change. Today would be the test to see if he could persuade his client to adopt certain business practices. To establish a brand, push a product, generate results and deliver success.

Success. Another word he never used to describe himself. But his business model would see success as a process rather than an end result, with every step counting.

An oval-shaped dirt parking lot came into view as Aiden drove to the beach. He brought the car alongside an adjacent wooden fence and took in the surrounding scenery. A small strip of sand lay between the grass and the shallow shoreline. Several other islands were in view, a few hundred feet across the sound.

He spotted a steel picnic table near the sand's edge. He sat down, placing a manila folder on top of the table. The folder contained several sheets of paper — project examples, resources on branding, placement and budgeting. He arranged them in separate piles.

Looked at his watch. Not sure why, since Onyx hadn't specified a time.

A grinding sound in the distance. Slowly getting louder.

Aiden turned around and saw Onyx roll in on his bike, hop off and walk to the bike stand.

"Well look what the cat dragged in," he said, saluting Aiden.

"Guilty as charged," Aiden replied with a smile.

The khaki-clad hippie walked over to the picnic table and sat himself across from Aiden, taking note of the papers on display.

"Looks like the newcomer is getting down to business."

"That's what we're here to do," Aiden responded, looking at the papers.

"Not to get too ahead of myself or rain on your parade," Onyx said, "but all I want is to get my stuff on some more shelves. I'm not looking to become some big-shot CEO."

"Not a big-shot. Just successful."

Onyx smiled.

Aiden grabbed the papers on his left and turned them toward Onyx.

"First thing's first: No one will remember you if your product isn't memorable. You're selling bags of spices – something most people think of as clutter in their kitchen cupboard."

"Well that's inspiring," Onyx said, shrugging.

"You're right," Aiden said. "It's not inspiring at all. If anything, it's insignificant."

He pulled out a piece of blank paper, wrote Onyx's name at the center and circled it.

"Who's this?" Aiden asked.

Onyx looked less than amused.

"Me," he said.

"And who's that?"

"Didn't I just answer that?"

"No," Aiden said. "You told me your name. Who's the person behind that name?"

Onyx scratched his left temple.

"I don't know, it's just me."

"What do people think of when they hear your name?"

"A rock?" he said with a smile.

"Seriously," Aiden said. "What makes you *you*?"

Onyx looked down, focusing his eyes on the table's rough surface.

He furrowed his eyebrows.

"Quirky," he said.

Aiden drew a line out from the circle on the paper, writing the word "quirky" at the end of the line.

He drew another line.

"What else?"

Onyx was catching on.

"A bit eccentric," he said. "Chill. Friendly. I guess I'm pretty typical of Cielo."

Aiden listened attentively as he copied all these words down on the paper diagram.

"What do your spices do for food?" he asked.

"They make the ordinary taste pretty good if you ask me," he said smiling. "Kind of a global variety. I guess it brings tastes from all over the world into your kitchen."

"Perfect," Aiden said, making more and more notes on the paper. "What kind of work does it take to get the mixtures right?"

"Lots of experimenting. Some failures, but a good product at the end."

Aiden made a few more notes and lines. Turned the paper around and pushed it in front of Onyx.

"This," he said, "is the brand of Onyx."

Onyx looked down at his name, slightly overwhelmed by all the adjectives protruding from the center.

"These are the things that make you different," Aiden said, "and will make your product stand out from all other spice mixtures."

"Wow," Onyx said, eyes widening. "That's good stuff!"

Aiden smiled. *"Good job, Mr. Lawrence,"* he said to himself.

"Good stuff, yes, but now we've gotta narrow it down." He handed Onyx the pen. "What are the biggest things that stand out?"

Onyx looked down again at the paper. He circled certain phrases. "Typical Cielo," "global variety," "eccentric," "friendly."

"Perfect," Aiden said. "This is the core of your brand. Global yet local, eccentric yet friendly. You already have your spice varieties nailed down. What we need is a brand name now."

Aiden put the paper aside and brought out another one with a bullet-point list.

"I did some brainstorming and came up with these initial options."

Onyx read the names. After only a few seconds he stopped looking.

"Global Rock Seasonings," he said out loud.

"You like it?" Aiden asked.

"I like the play on words. Cielo's a rock, so is my name. Global fair with a local connection. It's tight."

An applause erupted inside Aiden's head.

"You got it!" he said. "Short, yet memorable and effective. Now we move to production."

"Production?" Onyx asked.

"Vision won't go anywhere without some strategy," Aiden said, pulling out another sheet of paper.

"We've gotta get a logo designed for you. Here's a list of a few local artists, all priced out at their hourly rates." He put a second sheet beside it. "Here's a quote from a couple local businesses that can print your labels. Yes, you can get this stuff done off island for less money, but by promoting local businesses, it'll boost your localized appeal. Meaning you can charge more for your product."

"Dude," Onyx said, rubbing the back of his neck. "This is gonna be a lot of work."

"You'll have to put up some money at first, but you'll see a pretty good return on your investment.

Depending, of course, on where your product is placed."

He pulled out yet another sheet of paper.

"These are some stores on Sandman Island who might be willing to buy your spices. We've gotta convince them to buy it, but that'll be easy once we get the product finished."

Onyx glanced over the list of store names, eyes widening.

"This is great and all, Aiden," he said, "but I think you're making this into something bigger than it needs to be. I'm not interested in making tons of money off it."

"This isn't about making tons of money," Aiden said. "It's about getting yourself established and recognized."

"People already know me," he said. "This sounds a bit like a capitalist agenda."

"You could say that," Aiden said. "But we both know this could make you the next big thing on Cielo. Your name will be equated with excellence."

Onyx closed his eyes, then opened them.

He leaned back. "Excellence, huh?"

He smiled.

So did Aiden.

"What do you say then?"

"I say we do this," Onyx said. "What's my homework?"

"Check out the artists, choose one, set up a meeting and tell them about your brand. Once we get the visual down, we can move on to production."

Aiden stacked up his papers and gave them to Onyx.

Onyx smiled. "Looks like I'm sailing west toward the promised land, huh?"

Aiden nodded. "I think we both are. I'm all about forward motion now, my friend."

He looked up at his first client. "This is going to be good, Onyx."

Onyx winked. "It better." He then yelled out as he biked away. "If this goes under, you're the first person I'm coming after."

"Fair enough," Aiden shouted in response. He felt apprehensive about this project, but confident.

"Fair enough," he repeated.

* * *

For the first time, Aiden was on top of the world. He presented his ideas with smooth articulation and solid confidence. Maybe he could start his own consulting business after all.

Maybe even on Cielo.

He stayed at that picnic table for a couple hours, sketching out ideas and figuring out his next steps. Picking a company name, finding a rental space in town, ordering business cards.

The sun was starting to set in the west, the air cooling. Aiden decided he could finish back at the cabin; he wasn't about to lose any momentum.

He threw his stuff into the car and sped out of the parking lot, cruising down Canoe Drive. Turned off on a curvy side road. Fewer cars.

This Civic could turn on a dime. Left, right, left again. Aiden had mastered the art of speed, which came in handy on a road with so many bends and curves.

The next curve pointed Aiden straight toward the sun, blinding him and obscuring his depth perception.

As he fumbled for the sun visor, he saw a figure walking along the side of the road.

A deer, he assumed.

He slammed his brakes, no idea how far – or close – it was.

The brakes jammed, and the car began fish-tailing. Each attempt to correct the course saw sent the car spinning faster, spiraling across the road toward the deer.

His world slowed. He lifted a hand to block the sun's glare and saw the shape – the figure – as the car sped closer.

The deer only had two legs.

Was it even a deer?

Crash.

27. HARVESTING FATE

Aiden didn't know where he was. He woke to a crow perched on the Civic's hood. Screech after screech after screech.

Aiden slowly opened his eyes, winced upon seeing the sun through a shattered windshield. The crow walked across the hood and flew away, cawing.

"Where am I?"

Pain in his neck. Couldn't move much. Stopped trying.

Felt something drip down his head. Reached to feel it.

Blood.

A faint sound in the distance. Growing louder.

Sirens. An ambulance.

The passenger door had caved in completely.

His leg felt wet. He looked down.

More blood. Coming from his calf.

Two people jumped out of a vehicle and approached the smashed up car. He couldn't tell who they were and didn't know where they came from.

"We're on site," one said into a hand radio, kneeling down next to the car. "Male in his late 20s. Several surface wounds. Honda Civic wrapped around a tree by the ditch."

Paramedics.

"Will the driver's door still open?" the other asked.

A few clicks. "Yes."

He turned toward Aiden.

"Can you tell us your name, sir?"

Everything seemed foggy.

"Aiden," he said. "Aiden Lawrence."

"Memory seems to be intact," the first paramedic said. "Don't worry, Mr. Lawrence. We'll get you out of here. You're lucky to be alive."

"Can you remember what happened?" the other man said.

Aiden winced.

"I was driving along and got blinded by the sun," he said. "I saw something. A deer. Tried to stop but the brakes locked up and I started fish-tailing."

"A deer?" the first paramedic asked. "Did you hit it?"

"I think it was a deer," Aiden said. "I don't remember hitting anything, or even crashing."

The second man walked around the car, surveying the scene.

"Oh God," he said, his voice low and hollow.

"What?" the other asked. "Is it the deer?"

Silence.

"Wasn't a deer," he said, pointing to the tree on which the passenger door was plastered against. "Must've been a pedestrian. Woman. Mid 50s."

"Vitals?"

The paramedic shook his head. "None."

Aiden turned to the passenger door. He saw blood on the broken window.

It was on the outside.

Was it his blood?

He saw something between the door and the tree.

An arm.

A human arm.

Bruised.

Bleeding.

Wearing a gold watch.

He knew that watch.

"Dear God," he cried.

PART III

28. EAGER BUT FOR DAYLIGHT

Time stood still that week on Cielo.

Islanders went about their business somberly, never mentioning the tragedy but carrying it in their eyes.

They knew who died. They knew who killed her.

Not personally, but they knew enough. Some mainlander who moved to the island.

Who kept to himself.

Who violently wore out his welcome.

As the wind blew and the waves crashed at Sunset Strip, there was a stillness in the air. Not even the several hundred people gathered in the area added liveliness.

A minister walked toward the water's edge. He turned and faced the crowd.

"Who wants to be here today?" he asked, raising his right hand. "Surely there is plenty we would rather be doing. Anything to avoid the ugly reality behind today's gathering.

"Dearly beloved," he said. "To say that we have gathered here to remember and celebrate the life of Rosemary Friesen would be true, but it would not be comprehensive. My friends, we have gathered to grieve.

"So much of this story is tragic and ugly that it's best to start with what is good and beautiful.

"Rosemary passed many days at her cash register, always standing in the same place. Sliding grocery item after grocery item across a scanner in exchange for our cash. Extending kindness, never passing judgment.

"To be honest, such repetition would be enough to drive me – a minister of God's holy word – to doubt the purpose of my existence.

"One day, I decided to ask what made her keep coming back. I told her that I personally would wait in eager anticipation of the day's end. Her response? 'I am eager but for daylight.' She was eager for the coming day, for the promise of newness. To see each one of us walking through the store's doors. And she was eager to do it all over again every day.

"Rosemary faced significant abandonment in her own life, yet she used that pain to make sure we never felt abandoned ourselves. She thrived off the opportunity to influence – even just by saying hello at the cash register. It takes an extraordinary human being to maintain such perspective in the midst of monotony. We could always rely on her for guidance.

"My friends, we gather together today to mourn the tragic and, some might say, meaningless death of one of our dearest family members. And we grieve. I grieve. It's one thing to pass peacefully at life's natural end; it's another to be taken from this world so violently.

"I wrestled with God when I first heard the devastating news of Rosemary's death. I still wrestle. How could a person of such integrity be snatched away so quickly?

"But who am I to question? Who am I to know the measure of my days? Who am I negate the impact of Rosemary's legacy by becoming bitter?

"Rosemary wouldn't want us to wallow. She was guided by her faith, ever trusting that life extends beyond our time here. And she was eager to experience the better side of life when it was time. This was the final daylight she looked forward to.

"Do not be mistaken; I deeply grieve this loss. Every day that I walk into the store, I`ll think of Rosemary and her kindness.

"But while our loss is permanent, our grief needn't be. This day of grieving will come to an end at sunset, and a hole will remain in the heart of Cielo. But daylight is coming, my friends. It's coming before we know it; it came sooner than Rosemary expected. But she was waiting for it. She was eager. And when it arrived, she woke up in the presence of her Maker, hearing him say, 'Well done, my good and faithful servant.'

"I deeply struggled with what to say today. What not to say. Then I asked myself, what would Rosemary want to say to us? How would she want us to honor her passing? That conversation in the grocery store immediately came to mind, and her legacy became clear: be eager but for daylight."

29. A WRETCH LIKE ME

The crowd slowly dispersed, most people laying a white rose next to the recently placed headstone near the cliff's edge as a local singer sang "Amazing Grace" a cappella.

Aiden stood looking out from behind a tree, where he had observed the funeral from a distance.

Everyone knew who he was and what he did.

What did he do?

He killed Rosemary, crushing her between a tree and his car.

Old feelings of failure and condemnation crashed over Aiden. Only this time, it wasn't just in his head. It was on the front page of *The Cielo Platform*.

The 20-foot walk to the headstone felt like it took an eternity. When he finally stood over it, he offered the "goodbye" he didn't have the chance to verbalize.

His first funeral since Dad's.

Today, he actually grieved.

Tears poured from his eyes, dripping onto the headstone. Muffled cries escaped his pursed lips.

Rosemary was the closest Aiden had to a meaningful relationship. The only one, for that matter. She reached out when he needed it and led him to become the person he was today. Dad always offered it, but Aiden threw it back in his face. Mom never expressed affection to him; she didn't know how. So he shut her out to protect her and himself from the truth of Dad's death.

There was no hiding the truth behind Rosemary's death. He was visibly numb, but he writhed with pain. This time, no drink could drown out the fact that Aiden had robbed the world again.

First Dad, now Rosemary.

Aiden stood up and turned to walk toward the cliff's edge, the wind blowing in his face and drying his tears. He stopped one foot shy of the grassy ledge.

The pastor had talked about entering into God's rest. About being eager for the life that waits on the other side of earth. About faithfully enduring the storm.

Then there was that song.

"Amazing grace, how sweet the sound, that saved a wretch like me."

A wretch.

If God let a wretch like him take the lives of two saints, Aiden wanted nothing to do with this God. Nor should God want anything to do with Aiden.

The wind blew hard against the grass along the cliff's edge, sending dust and pollen up into the air.

He stepped closer to the edge of the cliff, remembering the first time he saw the waves crashing against the sharp rocks several stories below.

Then, fear had overwhelmed him.

Fear of death.

Of failure.

Of losing control.

Aiden rarely had the strength to take control. Whenever he tried, he lost.

Not today.

He leaned over the edge, breathed deep and looked up.

He was ready to jump. To escape the nauseating guilt that so strongly gripped his soul. To stop himself from taking another innocent life.

He closed his eyes and stepped out.

His whole body was jerked away from the edge by the collar of his shirt. He pivoted as he fell and landed face down in the dirt.

He turned, looking to see who had pulled him.

Chase.

No. He saw more than just Chase. He saw his own pathetic frailty in the face of menacing strength.

Emotional complacency towering over his own crumbling frame.

Personal choice defeated by inevitable fate.

Aiden had finally taken charge over fate and sought to end his pitiful existence. But he couldn't even do that.

Despair mixed with anger and quickly exploded into wrath as he looked into Chase's eyes. He lunged full force at Chase's midsection and tackled him to the ground, landing on the flat headstone and crushing the roses. He threw rapid punches through his tears.

"Go to hell!" Aiden screamed, summoning every remaining ounce of strength from within.

With one shove to Aiden's left shoulder, Chase threw him off and stood up. Entirely unaffected.

"You're not doing it," Chase said coldly. "You can't."

"What gives you the right to stop me?" Aiden demanded. He ran at Chase but was pushed to the ground before he could make contact, landing on his face again.

"Because you can't see anything for what it's worth," Chase said. "Jumping to your death is just a cop-out."

Aiden felt the blood rush to his face again as he pushed himself off the ground, giving him the strength to put Chase in his proper place.

"What good has life done for you?" he asked.

"What are you talking about?" Chase said.

"Don't even try to compare your situation to mine," Aiden said bitterly. "I killed my own father and now the closest I've had to a decent relationship. They weren't some crack heads who died of an overdose."

"What the –"

"I know who you are, Chase! Your parents killed themselves at your birthday party. God only knows the hell you went through, but you didn't let yourself feel *anything*! Look at you! I'm not going to become the cold-blooded bastard you are!"

Chase held his stare, not in the least affected.

"You're not so different from me, Aiden," he said.

His name, coming out of Chase's mouth for the first time, sounded like the scold of a father. Rebuke given in response to poor behavior.

"I don't want to be like you!" Aiden screamed, eyes wide and fists clenched. "You were abandoned by two losers; I killed two saints. Everything was taken from you; I'm the one who took everything away! I don't get another chance. Especially when it means turning into some monster that doesn't know how to feel. Because

192

what I feel right now is beyond grief and anger and disappointment - and I'm not living with it!"

"You really think your noble sacrifice will bring her back?" Chase shouted, pointing over to the headstone hidden beneath what remained of the roses. "You're pathetic, Aiden! You're weak! Rise up and be a man for once in your life!"

Aiden's eyes burned with rage; the veins in his neck throbbed.

"You think I can rise up? Look at me!" He threw his arms out. "I have nothing! I killed the one person who cared! I don't want to live in this God-forsaken world anymore! I don't deserve it!"

"Listen to me!" Chase scorned. "There's nothing noble in jumping! She was the one person who chose to point you toward something decent. You're just going to throw that all away? You're not fooling me, and you're not doing her any honor. You'll be more of a coward than you'll ever be a martyr!"

"And what honor did you bestow your parents?"

"They didn't deserve honor!" Chase yelled. "You think I don't know that I'm the result of cheap liquor and horny teenagers? There isn't anything to redeem about my past or my parents, and I wasn't about to offer them my condolence. You grieve when something good is lost. The world became a better place when they snorted that last line. They deserve the fate they got."

"And that gives you the right to dictate my fate?" Aiden asked, his voice breaking between cries. "Cielo is grieving, and it's because of me! I'm the one who crushed Rosemary's body between a car and a tree. I ended the life of an incredible human being. I'm the one who needs to pay!"

Chase threw his hands in the air.

"Stop making this about you, you selfish little prick!" he yelled, his voice bellowing. "You'll only be drawing more attention to yourself by jumping, and you're doing it to get what you want – sympathy. We don't have sympathy for you, Aiden!"

Chase held his gaze.

Painful silence filled the air between them, even as the wind blew. Waves crashed loudly against the rocks as the wind dictated the ocean's movement.

Chase turned and walked away.

"Do us all a favor and leave," he said, his back toward Aiden. "Don't go drawing more attention to yourself by jumping to your death. Just leave this island, and don't come back until you're ready."

Aiden was quiet, eyes wide, able to utter only a few words.

"Ready for what?" he mumbled.

Chase turned his head slightly.

"Ready to just walk," he said, his words quiet. "It's all we can really do."

Aiden dropped to his knees, clothes torn and eyes burning. Wishing that it was all over.

Wishing this day would pass.

He watched Chase walk to his truck in the parking lot. Waited until he was out of sight.

Then he cried.

30. GO EAST, YOUNG MAN

Two days had passed since the funeral. Aiden didn't waste one minute of it.

He packed up his belongings. Put a "For Sale" sign next to the cabin's driveway entrance. He was done. All he wanted to do was sell this cabin and heed Chase's advice: leave, and don't come back.

He was ready to take an eastbound sailing the next day back to the mainland. He'd catch a bus on the other side. Where he was heading, he didn't know. But he was leaving. Leaving this place called Cielo – this place that had become his hell.

Aiden had an upcoming court date regarding the accident. Likely to face charges for involuntary manslaughter, unsure of what the sentence would be.

Prison? Probably.

Probation? Certainly.

Whatever the charges, he would face the judge and pay his dues. Quietly, without bringing more attention to himself.

"You make for a quick exit," said a voice from behind him. Aiden turned, seeing Onyx in the gravel lot.

Aiden turned away; Onyx was a friend, but his presence brought no joy to Aiden.

"What are you doing here?" he asked in a muted tone.

"I think you gave me something by mistake," Onyx said, walking toward Aiden. He was holding out a folded piece of paper.

Aiden was weak, both physically and emotionally. He could barely stand under the weight of fury and turmoil.

But if taking this paper would rid him of company, he could summon the strength to do so.

He reached out for it and opened it.

Recognized it.

The letter he had written to Dad.

His shoulders tightened.

"Where did you get this?" he demanded, his voice shaky.

"It was in the folder with all the papers you gave me," Onyx explained.

Aiden realized he must have put it in there by mistake. Another humiliation.

"I'm leaving Cielo," he said. "Leaving and letting everyone grieve without me here. Just let it go."

"You going to see her?" Onyx asked.

"See who?"

"Your mom," he said. "She's still around, right?"

Onyx looked at the paper and spoke, reading a particular line aloud. *"Mom doesn't know any of this. I couldn't let her know."*

Aiden's jaw clenched.

"Don't step into this, Onyx," he said sternly. "You're the one friend I haveand I don't need this from you."

"Then I'm asking as your friend," Onyx said. "Are you going to see her?"

"She's the last person who needs to know about this."

"Seems like you've done that before, and it didn't leave you in good shape – judging by this letter."

"Judge all you want," Aiden said. "I'm not burdening her with this."

"With the truth? You've made a lifestyle out of burying the truth, man. Look at what it's done to you!"

Aiden was quiet. He didn't have another fight in him.

"Anyone who cares about me gets hurt," he finally said. "So do yourself a favor and stay away from me, Onyx. You owe it to yourself."

"And you owe yourself a lot more that whatever self-exile you're about to embark on. I know what I read in this letter. You burned your bridges with your Dad, and you're still flogging yourself over it. Doesn't sound like your Mom has too much longer. Don't let this end before you make it right."

Aiden said nothing.

Then he finally spoke.

"Chase told me to leave," he said. "That's all I can do. I'd only rub salt in everyone's wounds if I stayed here. I can't come back"

"You know you're not done with this place, with Cielo," Onyx said. "Maybe for now. But you don't have much left. Just your Mom. Cielo's one of the best places on earth, and it's waiting for you when you're done running."

Aiden hadn't looked up this whole time. His eyes remained fixed on the paper in his hand.

"I'll be here, man," Onyx said. "I'll always be here. But you've gotta take care of business first."

Business. Aiden thought back to their marketing strategy. Their plan for success and forward motion. Of reaching the promised land.

He scoffed out a desperate laugh. "So much for advancing to the unexplored west, huh?"

Onyx turned and started walking away from the cabin, looking at the "For Sale" sign. He kicked it.

"Sometimes you have to head back east before you can sail into the west – or at least pull up the anchor first."

31. SAILING AGAINST SUNRISE

It was early the next morning. Aiden walked down to catch the red-eye ferry. A thick fog obscured the views and delayed the boat's arrival. The boat could be heard in the distance, sounding its fog horn.

Other than the ferry, it was a quiet morning. Three seagulls perched along a nearby fence, peering down at the strip of sand, looking for breakfast. One flew over to the ferry terminal's deck and snatched up a few wayward sunflower seeds, likely left by a walk-on passenger.

Terminal.

Aiden remembered observing the word's double-meaning when he first came to Cielo with Dad so many years ago. The stopping-point of the ferry's journey and the end of a passenger's time on the island.

One building. Two endings.

The sun rose behind the mountains, burning away the morning fog and clearing the path for the boat that was pulling into the Cielo landing.

This boat was going east after leaving the island, taking Aiden back to his past. Away from serenity. Toward the courthouse.

This pending boat trip felt like he was being taken away to a death sentence after a grueling trial.

Cielo had been the mirror that revealed Aiden's depraved soul. It was his point of renewal. A source of community.

A glimpse of what life could be like.

What it should be like.

Ultimately, Cielo was the closest he had come to experiencing heaven.

But he wasn't suitable for heaven. It wasn't his time.

Not yet.

Here, he had finally made things right with Dad and yet single-handedly destroyed the very source of that inspiration. Another life taken; another wrong done.

A gentle breeze blew as a handful of cars drove off the boat.

He longed to arrive at an end.

To stop questioning his painful existence.

To live in perfect relationship with God, nature and others.

To be restored to the life his Maker originally intended.

To reach the final stage of this journey into the west.

His mind flashed back to Rosemary's funeral.

To the message.

The song.

That line.

"Amazing grace, how sweet the sound, that saved a wretch like me."

He knew needed that saving grace. He knew he needed it desperately.

He knew it was waiting for him.

What he needed first was some sense of reconciliation.

So he headed out of the island's eastern gate to where he needed to go. To Mom. To the last family tie that remained – a tie that was barely hanging by its last thread.

Following the ferry attendant's cue, Aiden boarded the boat, duffle bag in hand. He walked across the concrete boarding ramp.

The east gate closed, locking out any access to the island.

The ferry slowly pulled away from the dock. Aiden looked back as the engines roared and left a white trail of bubbles on the water's surface.

A small rainbow formed by the sun and lingered in the airborne mist as another deep honk from the fog horn alerted other boats to the ferry's presence.

Cielo gradually decreased in size with each passing moment. Houses became subtle dots along the water's edge, blurred against the trees. The island quickly grew indistinguishable from the others. Almost difficult to identify at this point.

He floated between two worlds, neither of which were desirable, neither of which could be called home. The one he was leaving held the promise of future rest; the one he was going to resounded with unfinished business.

A deep pain tugged Aiden back and forth between competing emotions.

Gratitude for his time on the island.

Remorse for how he was leaving.

Dread of the pending reunion with Mom.

Unsure of the words that would form.

Certain that pain would ensue.

Dead certain.

For the first time, Aiden was content being on public transit.

"Mommy!" he heard a young girl behind him – couldn't be older than six – running toward a green minivan. "I forgot my coloring book!"

He turned and saw the girl unlock and open the van's door with a remote key, grab a book and crayons, close the door and run back to her mother.

Aiden watched the child move swiftly in blissful ignorance, dirty blonde hair bouncing with each step. Unaware of any surrounding threats. Happy after her time on the island.

He grew envious of her joy.

"Maggie!" her mother yelled.

"What?"

"You need to lock it up again!"

The girl stopped in her tracks.

"Why?" she asked. "We didn't lock it back there." She pointed in Cielo's direction.

"Things are different now," the mother said, firmly grabbing her daughter's hand. "It's not as safe where we're going. People can steal our stuff if we leave it unlocked. Do you want your toys to get stolen?"

The young girl's eyes widened; she looked terrified by the thought of a thief breaking in and robbing her of her possessions.

"No," the daughter quickly replied, shaking her head.

The mother stooped down to her daughter's height and looked her in the eye.

"Trust is important," she said, "but we need to be safe. Do you understand?"

Joy faded from the girl's face. She glanced back at Cielo with deep longing before opening her mouth to speak. But the child said nothing.

She looked over at Aiden, locking her gaze with his. Both their eyes were wide but weary.

He knew how she felt.

He knew how she hurt.

She was sad.

Sorrowful.

Scared.

Painfully processing the transition from an oasis of peace back to a world of locked doors.

Aiden bit his lip and turned back to look at the distant islands.

"Don't worry," he heard the mother say, steering her daughter toward the elevator and pulling her into the realm of maternal safety. "We'll go back there again. Someday."

EPILOGUE

Against its will, all creation was subjected to God's curse. But with **eager hope**, the creation looks forward to the day when it will join God's children in **glorious freedom from death and decay**.

Romans 8:20-21*